HD

LOVE AMONG THE ARTS

When Stella Bates arrives at Minster House to take on the position of companion to the injured Lady Pamela Loates, she expects to live quietly in an outbuilding and focus on her photography. Soon, however, she finds herself looking after the two recalcitrant teenagers in the family, and it isn't long before the boorish attitude of Pamela's handsome son Rory softens into affection, and then love. But how long can Stella stay at Minster House, especially when she is being stalked by the sinister Buttonhole Man?

Books by Margaret Mounsdon
in the Linford Romance Library:

MARGARET MOUNSDON

◆

LOVE AMONG THE ARTS

Complete and Unabridged

LINFORD
Leicester

First published in Great Britain in 2013

First Linford Edition
published 2016

A catalogue record for this book is available
from the British Library.

ISBN 978–1–4448–2802–3

Published by
F. A. Thorpe (Publishing)
Anstey, Leicestershire

Set by Words & Graphics Ltd.
Anstey, Leicestershire
Printed and bound in Great Britain by
T. J. International Ltd., Padstow, Cornwall

This book is printed on acid-free paper

1

Stella Bates pressed her foot down on the accelerator. She hated being late. She peered through her windscreen as her wipers did their best to cope with the relentless rain. Lady Pamela said to take the first left after the filling station. The first left was a track classified unsuitable for vehicles.

Stella wound down her window as she spotted a young mother pushing a baby buggy. 'Excuse me. I'm looking for Minster House.'

The girl didn't bother to stop. 'First left past the garage.'

Biting down more frustration, Stella drove on. Orange forecourt lights loomed into view and opposite the second garage she spotted a left-hand turn. A grimy sign indicated it was Knight's Walk. Stella swung her car towards it, ignoring the protest from her suspension as it encountered the potholes. She pressed on, trying to imagine how many knights had ridden their steeds this way intent on wooing their lady loves. She hoped the ruts didn't dampen their ardour.

Stella had never liked February, and this year it was pulling out all the stops. Snow, frost, storms and a broken engagement; February certainly knew how to throw the book at her. Determined not to waste time thinking about Mark, Stella concentrated on the road.

The landscape stretched before her, bleak and rain-swept. Was she doing the right thing? Making the grand gesture was all very well, but if this arrangement fell through she was homeless.

She spotted a pair of wrought-iron gates displaying the name Minster House. She had arrived. Circling a small well, she came to a halt in front of a solid red-brick country house.

She leapt out of her car and tugged the old-fashioned bell pull. The door was yanked open with such force she nearly fell into the hall.

'Hello,' she said as she recovered her composure, 'my name is Stella Bates.'

'You're late.' The man's expression was decidedly unfriendly. 'Nearly an hour and a half late, to be precise.'

Stella did her best to smile. It wasn't easy when her teeth were chattering with the cold.

'Your services are no longer needed.'

'I beg your pardon?'

'Good day.'

'Now wait one moment.' Stella slipped her foot over the sill and winced as the edge caught the side of her boot. 'My interview is with Lady Pamela Loates. She didn't mention anything about a footman.'

The reference to a footman was a cheap jibe but it found its target.

'My name is Rory Loates,' he said in a cold voice. 'Lady Pamela is my mother.'

'In that case, would you please tell your mother I have arrived?'

'She doesn't want to see you.'

'Rory?' a voice called out. 'Is that Miss Bates? Show her in immediately.'

Seizing her chance, Stella sidled into the hall and hastened down the passageway, her wet boots squeaking on the polished flooring. Gently tapping on a half-open door, she poked her head round.

'Lady Pamela?'

A white-haired lady was seated in front of a log fire, one leg stretched out on a stool and covered with a light-weave blanket.

'Come in. That son of mine needs a lesson in manners. Fancy detaining you on the doorstep in this weather.'

'I'm sorry I'm late,' Stella began.

'Don't mention it. Rory,' she said to her son, who was now glowering at them from the doorway, 'we'd like some tea. You do drink tea, Miss Bates?'

'Indian if you have it; milk, no sugar.' Stella couldn't resist ordering Rory Loates around.

'Same for me please, dear.'

'You've already had your morning

4

coffee, Mother.'

'And now, as I have a guest, I'd like some tea. Off you go.'

For a second Stella felt sorry for Rory, until she remembered his treatment of her.

'Your son indicated that you'd changed your mind, Lady Pamela?' Stella began.

'Indeed I have not — and please, call me Pamela.' They smiled at each other. 'Rory is a stickler for punctuality. You are still interested in the position?'

Stella nodded. 'Perhaps I should tell you something about myself,' she suggested.

'I've already looked you up,' Pamela confided. 'Since I've been laid up after I twisted my ankle, I've had plenty of time to surf the net.'

'Is your leg very painful?' Stella asked.

'The swelling is going down. Rory's taken it upon himself to be my nursemaid but he's not very good at it. That's probably why he's so grumpy.

I'd been banging on about how clever I'd been, advertising for a companion without any family help and singing your praises. Then you let the side down by turning up late!'

'I'm really sorry.'

'Never complain or apologise,' Pamela twinkled back at her. 'That's what my father used to say.' She glanced down at a print-out in front of her. 'Your website shows an impressive list of qualifications.'

'Thank you.'

'I do envy your generation. Girls these days can do whatever they like. In my day, once you married that was it; at least, it was as far as I was concerned. I loved being a housewife and a mother. I had the best husband in the world too, but I had to rely on him for everything. My sister never married or had children and says she envies my life. I suppose the grass is always greener on the other side of the fence.'

From the kitchen they could hear the sound of rattling crockery. A log fell into the grate and created a shower of sparks.

'Would you like me to make up the fire?' Stella asked.

'That would be most kind of you. I always think there's something comforting about a real fire, don't you? Especially on a day like today.'

There was a bump in the doorway and Rory appeared with a tray of tea.

'Put it down there,' Pamela said. 'Stella will do the honours, won't you? She's very accomplished, Rory. Apart from her photographic qualifications, she knows how to make up a fire. What do you think about that?'

'I expect there's a lot about Miss Bates that would surprise me,' Rory replied.

Stella tried to convince herself that the flush on her cheeks was from the heat of the fire, but Rory's words stung. In any other circumstances they would have been bordering on an insult.

'Why don't you take yourself off somewhere, Rory?' his mother suggested.

'And leave me to have a private word with Stella.'

Rory hesitated.

'I think we can trust her not to make off with the teaspoons.'

Stella noticed the teaspoons were beautiful pieces of cutlery. The handles were engraved and had been polished until they shone.

'I'll be working on my car,' Rory replied with a brief nod at his mother.

'Poor old Rory,' Lady Pamela said after he left the room. 'He's used to having a team jumping to his every whim.'

'What does your son do?'

'I know one shouldn't boast, but I am so proud of him. He presents cutting-edge documentaries on television. I can't count the number of scoundrels he has exposed.'

'He's *that* Rory Loates?' Stella nearly dropped one of the engraved spoons in shock.

'You've heard of him?' Pamela looked inordinately pleased.

'I enjoy the programme, when I get the time to watch it,' Stella replied, reluctant to reveal she was one of its greatest fans.

'Rory avoids appearing in front of the camera if he can; that way people don't recognise him when he's on their tail.' Pamela patted a stool. 'If you've finished your tea, come and sit down beside me. I'm sure you've got lots of questions.'

'Your advertisement said you live alone,' Stella began.

'Rory has a rented flat in Poole about twenty miles away. He's staying over for a few days, as he's between assignments.'

'You have a daughter too?'

'June; she's two years older than Rory. She's married. Her children are called Tom and Fenella.'

Pamela's hand shook as she sipped her tea. Stella leaned forward and steadied the cup.

'Thank you. I know it's silly to get so emotional. The thing is, June and her husband . . . ' She hesitated. 'They're going through a difficult time. Andrew has moved to Dubai for six months. He's a contract engineer and they're having a trial separation.'

'I'm sorry.'

'These things happen. Anyway, the plan is for June and the children to move in with me.'

'And that was why Rory said you no longer need a live-in companion?'

Pamela held up a hand. 'Hear me out. I should have said that was the plan, but the family has gone down with a bug.'

Stella's reply was a cautious, 'I see.'

'June's plans to move here may come to nothing. She isn't the most reliable of people and she has let me down in the past. I wouldn't want to turn you away and then find she can't come and live me with either. So I'd like you to move into the byre. I know it's short notice.'

Stella hesitated. 'Isn't a byre a cow shed?'

Pamela's cheerful smile was back in place as she explained. 'Years ago this house was a working religious establishment. They kept cows and geese and grew their own vegetables. What was the byre has been converted into a self-contained unit. What I have in mind is for you to live there. That way we would be company without getting in each other's hair. I wouldn't want to interfere with your work. Of course, when I first made my plans I hadn't bargained on twisting my ankle.'

'Can you walk on it at all?' Stella asked.

'It's getting better every day, but you would be doing me the most enormous favour if you could take up my offer. I mean, I'm sure you've got loads of other places to see, and I appreciate life can be quiet around here. You probably want somewhere buzzing with wine bars and clubs.'

'I'm not really interested in that sort of thing anymore,' Stella admitted in a low voice.

'Mother?' Rory appeared in the doorway.

'Hello, dear. Have you finished changing your plugs, or whatever it is you do with that old car of yours?'

'I thought I heard the telephone. Didn't you?'

'I didn't hear it. Did you?' Pamela asked Stella.

She shook her head. She strongly suspected Rory of eavesdropping.

'We've finished our tea. Why don't you show Miss Bates the byre? She's going to stay with us. Isn't that good news?'

The look on Rory's face indicated that good news was the last thing he thought it was.

2

The extension was a short walk across a courtyard accessed from the back of the house.

Rory frowned at Stella's shoes. 'You'd better hang on to my arm if you don't want to slip.'

Rejecting his offer with a terse, 'I can manage,' Stella tottered after him across the cobblestones. The rain had eased and was now a gentle mist. The smell of wet earth helped clear her head and provided a refreshing change after the overheated atmosphere of Pamela's drawing room. Bright tubs of early spring flowers created a splash of colour against the drab walled courtyard.

'Are these buildings in use?' Stella indicated the double doors of the garages.

'Yes. I'm renovating a vintage car. My mother puts her hatchback in the end garage. She hasn't used it since her fall.

If you stay she'll probably ask you to drive it.'

They came to a halt in front of a solid oak door. Rory retrieved a key from under a flowerpot and inserted it in the lock. There was a satisfying click as he turned it.

'Why don't you want me to stay?' Stella blurted.

'Shall we just say, I know Mark Dashwood?'

A sharp intake of breath stabbed Stella in the chest. So that was it. After the break-up, Mark had circulated rumours about her being uncaring and unprofessional. The only weapon in Stella's armoury was to maintain a dignified silence. Her true friends didn't believe a word of Mark's fabrications about her temperamental outbursts being the reason he had gone back to his old girlfriend. If some people chose to believe what Mark was saying about her, then they were people Stella didn't care to associate with. Rory Loates would seem to be amongst their number.

'I have nothing to say on the matter,' she said. 'Now can we get down to business?'

She entered the sitting room. Stella suspected the cow byre had once been a gloomy place, but this room was bright and cheerful. Yellow curtains hung either side of the windows, letting in light and a fresh feeling of country air.

'My mother put a lot of effort into the refurbishment,' Rory said. 'It gave her a focus after my father died. She didn't want it standing empty, so I suggested that Aunt Doreen should move in.'

'Is that why you lied to me?' Stella asked.

'What?' Rory looked shocked by her question.

'You told me my services weren't required.'

'What I actually said was — ' Rory began.

'It doesn't matter. I got the general meaning.'

'I feel a member of the family would

be better suited to my mother's needs.'

'Have you any idea how pompous you sound?'

Stella was beyond caring what Rory thought of her. This man had made up his mind that she was an unsuitable companion for his mother without knowing the first thing about her.

'I don't think you realise the precariousness of your situation,' Rory retaliated.

'I've nothing to lose. You've made your feelings about me perfectly clear. So I'm returning the compliment. I don't particularly like your attitude either, and I cannot understand how a lady as charming as your mother could have such a boor for a son.'

'Wait a minute!' Rory's colour had now risen.

'No, you wait a minute. You've had your say, now it's your turn to listen to me.'

Stella had in the past been told her greatest fault was acting before she gave herself time to think. She knew that was exactly what she was doing now, but she was too wound up to care.

'Your sister is unable to move in for family reasons, and I don't see Aunt Doreen beating a path to your door, so I'd say I'm your only choice.'

'Doreen lives in Scotland.'

'What's that got to do with anything?'

'It's a big move to come south.' A fleeting look of distaste crossed Rory's face. 'And she and my mother don't exactly hit it off.'

Stella refused to be intimidated by Rory's uncompromising stance. 'Then you're stuck with me, aren't you? If it's any consolation,' she relented, 'your mother and I speak the same language. I like her and I think she likes me.'

'When could you move in?' Rory asked, displaying reluctant acceptance of the inevitable.

'Right now, if you like. I saw your mother's advertisement after I'd already given notice to quit my flat and the arrangement I'd made to move into rooms fell through. Lady Pamela invited me over for an interview. So there you have it. My work can take me out a lot during the day, but when I'm not on the road I hope to work here. The idea was that Lady Pamela and I could have supper together and discuss our day, unless we chose otherwise. You can't stay here forever, and with me on the premises you wouldn't have to worry about your mother.'

'Put like that, it does sound a good idea,' Rory acknowledged.

'I'm glad we agree on something.' Stella smiled up at him in the hope that Rory's expression would soften and he would smile back. Her hopes were dashed as he continued to frown at her.

'Would you be prepared to walk Sparky while my mother is incapacitated?'

'Sparky?'

'A russet-coloured spaniel of indeterminate pedigree. She was snoozing by the kitchen boiler when you arrived, otherwise I feel sure she would have made herself known to you.'

'I look forward to being introduced.'

'One more thing,' Rory began.

'I haven't got a police record, if that's what is worrying you. And as you know, I am not currently romantically involved,' Stella replied. 'I've got references in my briefcase which I can show you, along with my professional credentials and background checks.'

Rory seemed unsure how to react.

'I realise you're making a big decision,' Stella said in a softer voice. 'I promise you I will do nothing to hurt or upset your mother. Does that reassure you? In my defence, I can only add you shouldn't believe all you hear.'

'Miss Bates . . . Stella,' Rory said with the first faint suggestion of a smile, 'I was actually referring to my mother. What I want to say is, for all her refined ways she can be wilful. She doesn't always behave with the dignity one would expect from a lady of her years.'

'I'm beginning to like her more every minute,' Stella put in.

'Also, when my mother and her sister

get together they rub each other up the wrong way, and then there are fireworks. Once they didn't speak to each other for months.'

'The experience of working amongst models on a catwalk equips you for that sort of thing. And all sisters argue. It goes with the territory.'

'Then there's my sister. She can also be . . . ' Rory shrugged. ' . . . volatile.'

'What you are trying to tell me is that the Loates family is no different from any other. There's always someone not speaking to someone, but if anyone from outside threatens you then you'll stick together to a man?'

'I suppose I am,' Rory admitted.

'Then you're much the same as any other family.'

'You wouldn't mind getting the blame if things go pear-shaped?'

'All I can say is, as the outsider with a reputation, I promise not to stir things up.'

'You don't strike me as a lady long on patience.'

'Over the past few months I've had to harden up,' Stella admitted in a hollow voice, 'but I'd never vent my feelings on your mother.'

She looked down at the patterned carpet and missed the change of expression in Rory's eyes.

'Look,' she mumbled, tucking a curl of hair behind her ear, 'if you really don't want me here, would you make my goodbyes to your mother and thank her for the tea?'

'I made the tea,' Rory pointed out, 'so it's me you should be thanking.'

'I enjoyed your last programme,' Stella said, not knowing why she should admit such a thing to the man who had effectively dismissed her as unsuitable for the job in hand.

Rory looked gratifyingly impressed. 'Feedback is so important. What did you like about it?'

'That rogue landlord was making his tenants' lives unbearable, and he thought he could carry on getting away with it because he had half the local authorities in his pocket.'

'It was very satisfying to nail him,' Rory admitted.

They looked at each other in silence for a moment. It was Rory who spoke first.

'Why don't we try out the arrangement for a month? There is still my sister and her family to consider. They'll probably be in a better position in a month's time to make a decision.'

'It's a deal,' agreed Stella.

'In that case, welcome to Minster House.'

'I'd better get my things in from the car.'

'Drive it round the back. We only ever use the front door when we're entertaining. By the way . . . ' Rory paused. 'On a professional note, I'd be interested to see examples of your work.'

'Well, I have shed loads,' said Stella, and she started laughing.

'What's so amusing about that?' Rory frowned.

'It's how I started out,' she explained. 'My grandfather and his wife set up a shed erection business. I began photographing the finished product for my college coursework and they built up a brochure from my snapshots. When I realised people were buying sheds after looking at my photographs, I decided taking pictures was the life for me.'

'Is that what you do now? Sheds?'

'I'll photograph anything for anyone. I don't particularly like doing personal portraits because I find personalities get in the way, but the bills have to be paid and portraiture does pay well.'

'We haven't mentioned terms.'

'I thought it was bed and board in exchange for keeping a benign eye on your mother.'

'Is that what she offered you?'

'We didn't discuss details,' Stella was forced to admit.

After a short pause Rory said, 'I'm sure my mother would want me to honour that agreement.'

'Thank you.'

A feeling of relief swept over Stella. She hadn't wanted to return home to her grandfather, knowing how much he would worry about her not having somewhere of her own to live.

The buzzing of a mobile telephone interrupted them.

'Make yourself at home.' Rory said. 'Hello? Doreen? No need to worry, we're fixed. Her name is Stella Bates. Of course she comes with good references.'

She tapped him on the arm. 'I'll leave you to it.'

The patter of paws drew her attention to the doorway. 'You, I take it, are Sparky,' she said, bending down to pat the silky fur of the new arrival. 'How about we go for a walk and get to know each other?'

3

Stella had protested when Pamela insisted she use her car. 'I don't want the battery going flat on me. But I do need new windscreen wipers for my car,' Stella admitted.

'Problem solved.' Pamela passed over the keys.

The rainy weather had given away to gentle sunshine, and eager spring buds pushed through the wayside verges. Stella had been at Minster House for a week now. Rory had left the morning after her arrival. He'd tapped on her front door while she was having breakfast.

'Mother's still asleep. Could you look in on her later? Mrs Watts, the cleaning lady, is due around ten, and I think Mother would like to be up and dressed by then.'

Stella had watched him drive away

with an inward sigh of relief. She hadn't been looking forward to having him breathing down her neck.

There had also been a telephone call from his sister June. 'Sorry to land you in it,' she apologised. 'The children haven't been well and the last thing I would want to do is pass their germs on to my mother. How is she?'

After a quick update on the situation, June had asked, 'And my brother?'

'Fine.' Stella knew better than to tell June her first impressions of Rory.

'Don't take any nonsense from him,' June replied with a knowing laugh. 'Anyway, I'm glad you're looking after Ma. Any problems, you've got my number.'

'Now off you go, dear,' Pamela had insisted after Stella settled her down in the sitting room with a book. 'Have a good day. I look forward to hearing about it tonight. I'll ask Mrs Watts to get one of Rory's chicken casseroles out of the freezer. All we've got to do is pop it in the oven.'

'Rory can cook?' Stella couldn't conceal her surprise.

'He can do his own laundry too, and,' Pamela added, 'sew buttons onto his shirts. I wasn't having any of that nonsense about the little woman doing all that sort of thing. To keep things fair, I taught June how to change a plug and not to panic if the lights went out. I was on my own a lot when the children were young and it's amazing what you learn to do when you have to. Are you sure you're warm enough? That blouse is very pretty but rather thin.'

Assuring Pamela she didn't need a thermal vest, Stella set off for the day. Her commission was one she was looking forward to, and as she left the coast road she turned her attention back to the day's schedule.

Mr Jenkins's art gallery was situated on the outskirts of town. 'We're right next door to the community centre,' he had informed her. 'There's plenty of parking around the back. Don't use the showroom entrance. We keep it locked if we're not expecting visitors. You'll find me in the office.'

Stella found it with ease, and after fortifying themselves with coffee and biscuits Mr Jenkins suggested they start work.

'We're storing several important pieces of art on the premises, and I need to have them documented for insurance purposes.'

The workroom was a mass of bulky objects under dust cloths. In a far corner a team of workers was bent over a canvas.

Stella sniffed. 'What's that smell?'

'The fluid we use to dissolve grime. It's a lengthy process cleaning works of art, and it takes immense patience and dedication. I'm afraid I can't tell you any more.' Mr Jenkins tapped the side of his nose. 'Secrets of the trade.'

'If you'll show me the paintings you want photographed, I'll get down to it.'

Mr Jenkins had told her to take as long as she liked, so Stella settled down with her equipment in a quiet corner of the gallery. Outside she could hear the traffic trundling along the high street and the occasional mournful wail of a ship in the harbour. The day had started bright and sunny, but mist was creeping in from the sea.

Mr Jenkins poked his head around the gallery door halfway through the afternoon. 'How's it going?'

'I'm about done,' Stella replied.

'Actually, there's one more picture I'd like you to photograph. It's not part of the insurance assessment. It's outside in the car park. Would you mind?'

The picture was surrounded by portable lights and displayed on an easel. 'We had an interested party,' Mr Jenkins explained. 'Today was the only time he could view. As we didn't want to open up the gallery this was the next best thing. He has asked that we send him photographs.' Mr Jenkins glanced up at the lowering clouds. 'Do you think you can mange to take some before the rain sets in?'

The late request put Stella under

pressure. She didn't like working in half-light or moist weather conditions, but before she could voice her concern Mr Jenkins was called away by a member of staff. Taking several photographs in quick succession, Stella looked through her lens to take her last shot. A fat blob of rain landed on her hand. Fixing the flash as the sky darkened, she pressed her shutter before she realised in her haste she had also snapped two men in the background. One was wearing a warehouse overall and accepting a wrapped package from a flamboyantly dressed individual who was sporting a white rose in the buttonhole of the camel-hair coat draped around his shoulders.

The buttonhole man, alerted to her presence by the camera flash, looked in her direction. Mr Jenkins rushed out of the storeroom.

'Quickly,' he urged her, throwing a sheet over the painting, 'we need to get it inside.'

Deciding to crop her pictures later,

Stella packed up for the day.

'You can buy them from the corner garage,' Mr Jenkins advised when Stella expressed the hope that she hadn't left it too late to purchase her windscreen wipers.

Browsing through the motoring accessories shelves, Stella found what she was looking for. Standing in the queue to pay, she caught sight of the same man she'd seen wearing the camel-hair coat outside Mr Jenkins's gallery. The white rose in his buttonhole was unmistakeable. She waited for the right moment to raise her hand to attract his attention in order to apologise for her earlier intrusion on his privacy, but before she could do so she was pushed to one side as an assistant rushed past her.

'Hey, you!' he shouted as the man got into his car and drove off.

'I've got his registration number,' the cashier called out to the assistant who failed to stop him.

'What's happening?' Stella asked as she reached the desk.

'Customer drove off without paying,' the cashier said as he rang up her purchases. 'It makes me so cross when they do that. It's probably a hired car, too, so we won't be able to trace the driver.'

Stella wondered if she should mention having seen the driver at Mr Jenkins's gallery.

'Want the whole aisle, do you?' an impatient customer asked. 'Only, some of us need to get to the pay desk.'

Stella mumbled an apology and pocketed her receipt before moving out of his way.

* * *

'I filled your car with petrol,' she explained to Pamela over their chicken casserole supper. The two women sat at a scrubbed pine table dipping chunks of home-baked bread into the last of the sauce.

'That wasn't necessary, dear.'

'The inland route is significantly

longer than the coast road, and it was too misty to take that.'

'It's not your fault the weather deteriorated, but I appreciate the gesture. Do you fancy ice cream? I always keep a tub in the freezer, and some shortbread biscuits in the cupboard for the grandchildren. We can have dessert in the sitting room while you tell me about your day.' She looked around for her crutches. 'I would offer to help but I'm afraid I might drop something.'

'You sit down by the fire,' Stella insisted. 'I'll be with you shortly.'

'You must have another shortbread biscuit to go with the last of your peach and pecan ice cream,' Pamela urged. 'You didn't have any lunch, did you?'

Stella remembered the bar of chocolate she'd bought at the garage; but after the incident with the man in the camel-hair coat, she had forgotten to eat it.

'You need one good meal a day and I'm determined to see you get it.'

'That wasn't the idea,' Stella insisted.

'I am supposed to be your companion.'

'That's exactly what you are, dear. That wretched doctor says I've still got to rest up for a few more days. I've done all the crosswords in the newspaper and watched more television than is good for me, so I'm ready to hear about your day.'

It was past midnight before Stella was ready for bed. Sparky had been clamouring for a late-night walk and had promptly run through as much mud as she could find. By the time Stella had cleaned her paws, settled her and Pamela down for the night, unloaded the car and put all her gear in the study, she didn't know if she could stay awake long enough to enjoy a bath. Opting for a warm shower instead, she sat on the bed and checked through the day's voice mail.

'Hello, darling.' She listened to Amy's voice and smiled. Amy was her grandfather's second wife. They had married when the eleven-year-old Stella had come to live with her grandfather after the deaths of her parents. It had at the time been more of a marriage of convenience, but over the years it had developed into a deep abiding love. Jim had needed help looking after his distraught granddaughter; and Amy, with a grown-up daughter and two sons of her own, had taken on the duties of a step-grandmother with her customary cheerful efficiency.

'Jim and I have been inundated with queries now the lighter nights are here and people are thinking about their gardens again. When are you coming to visit? Don't leave it too long. Love you. Bye.'

Flicking down the list of calls received, she frowned at a number she did not recognise. After her break-up with Mark she had changed her mobile number. Only a few people were in possession of her new details.

'Miss Bates? I don't like my photo being taken without my permission and I want all the copies and the original destroyed.'

Stella sat on the bed doing her best not to shiver. The cultured tones suggested he was the man with the white-rose buttonhole. Stella was normally scrupulous about invading an individual's privacy and she knew she must apologise for her lapse in professionalism, but all the same she didn't like being threatened.

Her fingers hovered over redial. It was late and she was tired. She didn't want to return the call until she'd had more time to think things through. The menacing tone of the call left her feeling uneasy, and how had the caller obtained her personal number? And then there had been that business at the petrol station. Did she really want to get involved with such an individual? If she didn't reply, perhaps he might think he had got the wrong number and let the matter drop.

Stella switched off her mobile and went to bed. It was several hours before she fell into a troubled sleep.

4

Stella was looking forward to a quiet weekend. With June coming to visit her mother, there would be fewer demands on her time.

On the Saturday morning she only half-registered the comings and goings in the courtyard: loud voices, barking, car doors slamming.

The painting on the easel hadn't been easy to shoot; and due to the rain Stella had taken her pictures in a hurry, setting her camera at as wide an angle as possible. She now saw that the two men talking together featured in three of her shots. In two they were shadowy background figures, but in the third their heads were bent close as a package changed hands.

Stella still hesitated about returning the call. There had been no further communication from the man with the buttonhole. It would be difficult to identify either of them from the photo as their faces were partially obscured. The only distinctive feature was the buttonhole in the camel-hair coat.

A furious hammering on her door made her jump. She now realised the level of activity outside was rather more than that associated with a simple day visit from the family. A white van was parked across the kitchen doors and items of furniture were being carried through into the main house.

'Stella?' A blonde woman stood on the doorstep. She was wearing a fluorescent blouse of headache-inducing colours, and black leggings. 'Hi. June Waugh.'

'You don't look like Pamela,' Stella said, then apologised. 'Sorry, that was rude of me.'

'That's because I'm adopted. After years of marriage Ma didn't think she could have children, so they adopted me. Two years later Rory was a big but welcome surprise. Lovely to meet you. Sorry about the racket.' June gestured over her shoulder. 'We're moving in.'

Stella's smile of welcome froze. 'I thought Pamela said you were only coming for the day.'

'That was the original plan. Don't worry, you're not being evicted. Actually, you might decide to go anyway after I tell you what's going on, but I hope you'll stay. Your being here has perked Ma up no end.'

The sight of an impressive-looking music system diverted Stella's attention.

'The children wouldn't be parted from their favourite things so we hired a man with a van, bundled it all in, and here we are. It's going to be cramped, but they won't mind.'

'Are you sure you don't want to move in here? It would be much more comfortable and make for a degree of privacy.'

'The children want to stay in the main house. They've sorted out their bedrooms already.'

'Where are you going to sleep?'

June trilled with laughter. 'I'm not moving in. I'm moving out — to Dubai.

Andrew, my husband, has asked me to join him. It's complicated, but there's a chance we could be getting back together. Obviously we don't want to disrupt Tom and Fenella's schooling. They board during the week and will only be around at the weekends. It was all done in a hurry; that's why Ma didn't have time to tell you anything.'

'I see.'

'Please say you'll stay. I know this is more than you bargained for, but they are good children and they won't give you any trouble.'

'I hate you!' a teenage girl screamed at a younger boy who was running away from her, waving a mobile phone at June.

'Fen's got a text from gruesome Gloria. They think Mr Thomas is cool.' He made an unattractive choking noise. 'He teaches art and wears a stupid smock and he never washes his hair.'

'Give it back.'

The two of them were now engaged in an unseemly tussle.

40

'Don't you just hate it when your children do that? You praise them to the skies and they let you down. Embarrassing or what?' June raised her eyebrows but made no attempt to part the warring twosome. 'Do you have children, Stella?'

'Not yet.'

'Very wise. I suggest you think long and hard before you do. Tom, stop that and come and introduce yourself to Miss Bates.'

'Stella, please,' she insisted.

Tom flashed her an impish grin. 'Hi, Stella,' he said. 'I'm Tom. I'm nearly thirteen. This is my sister Fenella. She's fifteen, and I quite like her at times.'

Fenella was busy tucking her shirt back into her jeans and attending to her hair. She glared at her brother and snatched her mobile out of his hands.

'Fenella,' her mother said in a sharp voice, 'Miss Bates is waiting to be introduced.'

'Hello,' she said in a sulky voice. She turned to her mother. 'Why do you always take Tom's side?'

'I don't, darling.'

'Yes you do. My things are private. He had no right to take my phone.'

'Who wants to read your soppy texts anyway?' Tom began to cough.

'I think we'd better go back inside,' June insisted. 'There's a sharp wind and we don't want the pair of you catching another bout of flu.'

'Do you need any help?' Stella asked.

'Not necessary,' June assured her. 'I'll be off shortly. My flight leaves at five. If I don't have time to say goodbye, then I'll see you sometime; not sure exactly when.'

A forlorn Sparky trailed over to nuzzle Stella's legs. 'Fancy a walk?' she asked. Sparky's tail wagged tentatively. 'Away from all the chaos, yes?'

★ ★ ★

By the time they returned, the white van and June had gone. In the background Stella could hear the thud of loud music. Sparky whined.

'It looks like we could be in for a rough ride,' Stella said as she discovered the remains of a scratch lunch on the kitchen table. 'Pamela?' she called through.

She tiptoed into the sitting room to find Lady Loates fast asleep in an armchair. Picking up Pamela's tea tray, she made her way back into the kitchen. The floor felt sticky and she trod on something crunchy.

Following the thud of heavy metal, she climbed the stairs. The two bedrooms Fenella and Tom had chosen were at the end of the corridor. Striding into the first one, she turned off the music.

'Hey,' Fenella protested, screwing the lid onto her nail varnish and then inspecting her phone for messages. 'I was listening to that.'

'So was half the county. Where's Tom?'

'Next door I 'spect.'

'Fetch him, please.'

43

Something in the tone of her voice told Fenella that Stella meant business. A few moments later Tom ambled in.

'What's that noise I can hear?' he demanded with his infectious grin.

'It's called silence,' Stella replied.

'How'd you get her to turn it off? She never does what I tell her.'

'I don't take orders from a kid brother.'

'Ground rules,' Stella interrupted them before another argument developed.

Two pairs of eyes swung in her direction.

'You what?' Tom demanded.

'You clear up the kitchen after you've used it.'

'That's Mum's job,' Fenella replied.

'She's not here, and I have no intention of running around after you. Neither has your grandmother, whose hospitality you are abusing.'

'I haven't abused anyone,' an indignant Tom protested.

'You are to make your own beds and

keep your rooms tidy. Laundry is to be taken down to the washing machine and not left on the floor.' Stella glanced down to a discarded T-shirt and a pair of tights. 'Do I make myself clear?'

'You're only the hired help.'

'Fen,' Tom said, his face creased up in concern, 'that's not polite.'

'I agree with you, Tom. Unless the kitchen is spotless by this evening there will be no supper. Do I make myself clear?'

'This is worse than being back at school,' Fenella grumbled, stooping down to pick up her tights.

'I'm sure arrangements could be made for you to board full-time,' Stella replied. She wasn't too sure where she stood on that one, but her threat had the desired effect.

'Come on, Tom.' Fenella grabbed up her dirty T-shirt. 'Best do as she says.'

'You wouldn't really forget about supper, would you, Stella?' he asked with a concerned look. 'We only had toast and jam for lunch, and Fenella burnt the toast. I'm ever so hungry.'

Stella's heart melted. 'How about we cook a sponge cake?'

The baking session turned into a hit and tea consisted of crumbly tarts soggy with raspberry jam; a sponge that wasn't exactly fluffy but satiated teenage appetites; and an apple tart, the remainder of which was put by for Sunday lunch.

Much refreshed after her snooze, Pamela was pleased to have her grandchildren's company, and the evening ended in a noisy board game followed by a late-night supper of pasta and cheese sauce. Stella wasn't too sure the children's nutritional requirements had been met by their day's rather stodgy diet, but she had been too busy to pay much regard to vitamins.

'How do they get back to school?' Stella asked as she and Pamela indulged in a glass of wine after the children had gone upstairs.

'Would you mind?' Pamela asked after a short pause. 'St Matilda's isn't far away. As soon as I can drive again I'll do the honours, of course.'

'It's half term,' Fenella announced from the doorway. 'Had you forgotten, Nan?'

'I'm not sure that I ever knew,' Pamela replied with remarkable composure.

'We'll be home all week.'

Stella's heart sank. There was no way she could leave Pamela on her own with a pair of active teenagers.

'I'm just taking these through to the washing machine,' Fenella informed Stella, holding up what looked like a department store full of clothing. 'I'd like to wear my pink top and jeans tomorrow.'

Deciding that Fenella's next lesson would be how to colour-code her washing, Stella heaved herself out of her chair. 'I think we're going to have to increase our catering order for this week,' she informed Pamela.

'Thank heavens for online deliveries.' Pamela also stirred herself. 'Have you seen my laptop anywhere?'

'Stella!' came a wail from the kitchen. 'I think I've pressed the wrong knob on the washing machine. We've got a flood.'

5

'Don't fiddle with that.'

'Only wanted to see what other jobs you've got on.' Tom was busy scrolling through Stella's messages.

'Do as Stella says,' Fenella ordered him from the back seat.

Ever since they'd cleared up the flooded kitchen together and Stella had unblocked the outlet hose, she and Fenella had become firm friends.

'That was really awesome,' Fenella enthused as she'd poured away the last bucket of water while Stella finished mopping the floor. 'When I get back to school I'm going to do a presentation on it.'

'Clearing up a flood?' Stella stretched her aching back and squeezed out the sponge.

'We always have to tell everyone how we've spent our half term. It's part of our public speaking skills. Bet none of the others will have done anything like this.'

Stella hoped there would be no other disasters for Fenella to report back to her school friends. It wasn't the experience of a lifetime to learn that the details of your in-house dramas might be posted on the web.

'Read out the directions to the catering college,' Stella suggested to Tom in an effort to distract him from playing around with her mobile.

'Left at the lights,' he said.

Fenella rubbed away a patch of condensation on the window and stared out at the rain pounding the pavement. 'My hair will go fuzzy,' she complained, 'and I spent ages straightening it.'

'Your dryer flicked the lights again this morning,' Tom informed her. 'Mum's told you to get a new one.'

'Can't afford it, and it isn't my birthday for ages. Will you buy me a new one?' she asked Stella.

'Not right now,' Stella replied.

Fenella changed tack. 'I hope Sparky will be all right at the vet's.'

'She was probably sick from something she ate.'

'Green,' Tom said through a mouthful of chocolate as the lights changed colour. 'Go past the supermarket for about half a mile. The college is on the right.'

'There it is.' Fenella leaned forward. 'Why do people want photos of cakes?'

'It's to advertise their catering course. Do you want to stay here or come with me?'

Tom and Fenella opted to accompany Stella inside.

'Remember, you are on your best behaviour,' Stella warned them. 'I can't have you compromising my professional integrity.'

'Oooh.' Tom made a face. 'Does anyone know what you're talking about?'

'I'm serious,' Stella said. 'Carry this and don't drop it.' She thrust a tripod at Tom and gave Fenella a bag to hold.

The morning went well. Fenella

displayed a talent for imaginative display, and Stella let her help set up one of the scenarios.

'Are those cakes real?' Tom asked as Stella took her final photo.

The college principal, who had arrived to see how they were getting on, answered his question. 'They are indeed, young man. Freshly baked today. You can take your pick.'

'Only two,' Stella said to the pair, remembering the chocolate bar and fizzy drink Tom had already consumed in the car.

The principal thanked Stella when the session was over. 'I look forward to seeing the proofs. We need the pictures for the autumn prospectus.'

'Thank you for being so accommodating about the children.'

'At the risk of being labelled a sneak, I should tell you your children have each eaten two cakes.'

Tom's cheeks bulged as he hurried to swallow the last of a chocolate roll. 'You did say we could take two,' he pointed out.

'I meant one each.' Stella looked at an equally guilty Fenella, who was licking sponge-cake icing off her fingers.

She widened her eyes. 'It's been hours since breakfast. And I only had a small bowl of cereal.'

'That's because you were late getting up and doing your hair,' Tom replied.

'No harm done,' the principal smoothed things over. 'I'm glad you both liked the cakes. I may call on you for an endorsement.'

'What's that?' Tom demanded.

'A recommendation.'

'Does it mean we get to eat more cakes?' he asked.

'I see you've a budding businessman on your hands,' the principal said with a smile.

'Come on, you two. Help me pack up then we'll be off to the vet's.' Stella hustled them out of the kitchen.

'Why does this man keep leaving nasty messages on your voice mail?' Tom asked. He was now seated in the back of the car and was again scrolling through her messages. 'He says he wants the pictures back or it'll be the worse for you.'

'Turn it off, now,' Stella snapped. 'And you're not to touch my mobile again, either of you. Do I make myself clear?'

Two subdued voices indicated agreement.

'It's a case of respecting other people's property,' she said, attempting to soften her words.

'There's the vet.' Fenella pointed to a white-coated figure emerging from the practice holding a cat box.

The two anxious youngsters leapt out of the car and raced towards him. 'If you'll settle up with the nurse, Mrs Waugh,' he said, beaming at Stella, 'you can take Sparky home with you.'

'That's the second person today who thought you were our mother,' Fenella giggled, linking her arm through Stella's. 'You must be looking extra old.'

'Perhaps it's you who's looking like a child,' Tom teased.

'Come on,' Stella coaxed Fenella out of a potential sulk, 'let's go home and have some tea.'

With Sparky gently snoring in her basket by the boiler and Tom and Fenella happily sparring over what television programme they were going to watch, Stella took the opportunity to escape to the cow byre to get some work done.

She played back the messages on her mobile. Making a note to contact the art gallery in the morning to see if Mr Jenkins knew anything about the incident, she heated up a tin of her soup.

Opening the back door, she inhaled the velvety scents of honeysuckle mixed with rain-washed grass. Mark had never liked the great outdoors.

Stella realised this was the first time she had thought about Mark Dashwood for days. He belonged to another life. She perched on a dilapidated seat and sipped her soup with a satisfied sigh.

She wondered if anyone had updated Rory on developments at Minster

House. June had mentioned Andrew's tour of duty was for six months. At the end of that period it would be time to take stock of the situation. Meanwhile, Stella was content to stay put.

'Stella?' she heard Tom calling her name. 'Fenella's fused the lights. The house is in darkness. Nan can't move in case she twists her ankle.'

'Where's the fuse box?' Stella demanded as Tom dragged her across the court-yard.

'Don't know.'

'Go and ask your grandmother and find a torch.'

'It's upstairs.' Tom was waiting for Stella as she manhandled a stepladder through the back door. He waved a torch at her. 'I found this but the battery's flat.'

'Does Pamela have a spare battery?'

Tom raced off again to find out.

Fenella leaned over the banister. 'Can you see where you're going?'

'I expect it's only the trip switch.' Stella manoeuvred the steps into place.

'Hold this thing steady for me.'

'Where's Tom?' Fenella asked.

'Looking for a torch battery.'

'I've got a meditation candle in my room.'

'We don't want naked flames about the place. It's too risky.'

'I'll be careful.'

Fenella shielded the flickering flame with her hand. 'We ought to see if Tom's found another battery.'

'I haven't,' his voice floated up the stairs, 'and Nan says she forgot to get a spare. Can I help?'

'Hold this up so Stella can see what she's doing.' Fenella passed over the candle.

Stella felt her way along the line of switches. 'I'm going to reset the trip. Ready?'

'It's still dark down here,' Tom complained when nothing happened.

'Give it another go,' urged Fenella.

'Brace your body against my legs.' Stella pushed hard down on the switch. 'It's really stiff.'

A loud bark from Sparky caused Stella to lose her footing. Fenella shrieked as Stella's foot squashed her fingers. The stepladder swayed.

'Look out!' Tom dropped the candle onto the carpet.

Rushing to help, Fenella relinquished her hold on the stepladder. Stella felt it wobble under her as the landing was bathed in bright light. The smell of singed carpet made her eyes water.

'Shut up,' Fenella shouted at Sparky, 'and get out of the way.'

'What's going on up there?'

Feet pounded the stairs as Tom banged a book down hard on the candle in an attempt to dowse the flames. Stella lost her last hold on the stepladder and fell off straight into Rory's arms.

6

Rory Loates strode across the court-yard.

'Do come in,' Stella invited. 'I wouldn't want you to graze your knuckles hammering on my door. Come through to the kitchen. Coffee?'

'What exactly is going on?' he demanded.

Stella took a deep breath. 'Your sister has flown out to Dubai to join her husband.'

'I know that.'

'I have been helping your mother look after the children.'

'Why wasn't I told about this?'

'That's something you must take up with June.'

'Tom tells me you've been getting threatening messages.'

'That has nothing to do with the situation here.'

'I can't have members of my family threatened by your shady connections.'

'They haven't been threatened by anyone. You wouldn't have known about it if Tom hadn't been scrolling through my messages.'

'It's as well he did.'

'Do you normally encourage your nephew to pry into other people's private correspondence?'

'This is different.'

'It seems you have one rule for your family and another for me.'

'We're wandering off the point.'

'I totally agree with you, but as you don't seem to be in the mood to listen to anything I have to say, why don't you carry on with your unfounded accusations? I'd be interested to hear what else you are going to blame me for.'

Rory was breathing as heavily as Stella. After the damage to the carpet turned out to be no more than a nasty scorch mark and the excitement had subsided, the children were dispatched to bed. Stella had made her goodnights and left Rory to catch up with his mother.

'The house is in chaos and my mother is exhausted. She tells me the kitchen has been flooded. The dog has been poisoned. Fenella and Tom are running wild on a diet of chocolate, cakes and fizzy drinks. And if that isn't bad enough, you expose the family to further danger by fusing the lights and nearly setting fire to the house by dropping a candle onto the landing carpet. I don't think I've forgotten anything.'

Stella clenched her fists. Never in her life had she so wanted to throw a punch.

'For a start I did not fuse the lights.' She stopped speaking. It wasn't in her nature to tell tales, and she was adult enough to realise that whatever she said would make no difference.

'My family's welfare is my main concern.'

'When your sister left the children here without any warning, I offered

61

them the use of the cow byre, but Tom and Fenella wanted to stay in the main house. They're responsible enough to realise what's going on and responded to the situation positively. I can assure you they are in no danger from me or my so-called shady connections.'

'I want you to leave,' Rory said.

'Good idea.' Stella got to her feet.

'Where are you going?' Rory looked her up and down in surprise.

'Devon.'

'Hang on a moment.' Rory put out a hand to detain her but Stella stepped away from him.

'Fenella hasn't quite got to grips with the washing machine. Tom doesn't like broccoli, and if you try to make him eat it he has a violent reaction. I don't think there's anything else, but as you're such an expert in emergency situations I'm sure you'll pull it all together.'

'You can't leave without giving notice.'

'Then sue me.' Stella couldn't resist

adding, 'But remember, I have shady connections.'

'I have to be in London next week for an important interview.'

Stella's outrage diluted into amusement. 'Oh dear.'

Rory was beginning to realise that he had painted himself into a corner. 'Perhaps we could come to some sort of arrangement?' he offered.

'Some people never listen, and you are one of them.'

'I spend my working day listening to what people have to say.'

'It's a pity that business practice doesn't extend to your private life then, isn't it? A man as resourceful as you shouldn't find domestic life too much of a challenge. Enjoy. I'll come back for my things, shall we say in a week's time?'

'You can't leave.'

'You're repeating yourself. You've told me to go and I'm obeying orders. Goodness knows what I'd get up to if I were left in charge one day longer. I'd be amazed to find the house still standing.'

Tom raced through the front door. 'Hi, Stella, will you help me load my new video game?'

'Can't you see I'm busy talking to Stella?' Rory stalled him.

'Fen's done it again — fused the lights,' Tom informed them. 'And there's a horrid smell coming from her hairdryer. I think it's going to go up in flames. Sparky's been sick and it's Fen's turn to clear it up, and Nan wants to know if you'll drive her to the surgery — and I nearly forgot, Rory, there's someone on the telephone for you. He says you're needed in London right now.'

Stella smiled at him. 'I'll pop the keys through the letterbox when I'm done here.'

'Where are you going?' Tom demanded.

'I'll be away for a few days.'

'You will come back, won't you?'

'That all depends on Rory. By the way,' Stella called after Rory, 'there aren't any batteries for the torch, so you may need to borrow Fenella's candle if you have to reset the trip switch.'

'Of course you can come down.' Amy sounded delighted to hear from Stella. 'You're overdue a visit. Actually,' she added, lowering her voice as if she didn't want to be overheard, 'there's something we need to discuss.'

'It's not Granddad?' Stella asked in concern.

'No, nothing like that,' Amy assured her. 'I'll make up your bed in your old room. If you can't find us in the cottage we'll be up in the workshop.'

Stella thrust a few essentials into an overnight bag. She wished she had time to explain to Pamela her reasons for leaving, but if she lingered any longer she suspected the children might talk her into staying.

Zipping up her bag, Stella hefted it out to her car and tossed it in the boot. Then she scribbled a note saying she would be back to collect the rest of her things as soon as possible. Not wanting to be accused of taking property that wasn't hers, she added a postscript explaining that the key to the study was in the desk, but she would be grateful if the door wasn't unlocked because it would disturb her work in progress. She promised to vacate the property at the first opportunity.

Sparky trotted across the courtyard and sniffed at Stella's shoes.

'Hello,' she said, patting the animal's head. 'Are you feeling better?'

Sparky made snuffling noises, then went off to investigate any overnight activity.

Stella poked her head round the kitchen door. The milk was on the table and already beginning to go off. Someone had left the fridge door open, and she could hear an unattractive noise coming from the washing machine.

Quickly depositing her letter under a cold mug of coffee, Stella made her exit. Jumping in her car, she started up and headed for the main road.

7

Stella hummed as she drove along. The prospect of seeing her grandfather and Amy always lifted her spirits. They had been together for thirteen years now. It was a second marriage for them both; and although their relationship could never be classed as a grand passion, they were happy and had provided the solid family background Stella desperately needed.

Stella's charity-worker parents had died in South America in circumstances never wholly revealed to her. She had been at school in England, a troublesome adolescent who had gone off the rails when the news had been broken to her. Rebelling against authority had been the only way she could release her grief, and if it hadn't been for Amy's unending patience she wasn't sure what would have happened.

Amy had been widowed for many years and she had met Jim when she had taken on the job of his business assistant. When he had proposed he had made it clear that Stella would be a permanent part of their new life together. He too was grieving over the loss of his daughter and son-in-law and knew the change it would make to all their lives. Their marriage had been a quiet church ceremony with Stella as bridesmaid and one of Amy's sons as best man.

Amy had treated Stella as her own granddaughter, and as such Stella loved her as she would have loved her real grandmother. Over the years Amy's and her grandfather's feelings for each other had deepened into love. They shared private jokes, worked together every day, and hated being apart. Amy never lost her temper, despite the provocation Stella had caused her in the early years of her marriage.

Amy and Jim lived in a fisherman's cottage a few miles along the coast from

Clovelly and ran their shed erection business from premises at the far end of their village tucked away behind a quiet bay, situated on a part of the coast overlooked by tourists.

Shed and outbuilding erection was hard work. Stella remembered helping Amy and her grandfather treat the wood that would soon deteriorate in the salty climatic conditions if it were not weatherproofed. With their pots and brushes they would set to, Jim singing loudly and out of tune until Amy told him to keep quiet as he was upsetting the neighbours.

Stella inhaled, convinced she could smell the sea even though she still had twenty miles to go. She pressed on, keen to put as much road as possible between herself and Rory Loates.

She felt a twinge of conscience. Perhaps she shouldn't have walked out, but Rory had accused her of putting the lives of his family in danger.

Although her mystery caller had discovered her telephone number, he would have had no idea of her address. She would not have liked Rory's family to be placed at the mercy of such an unpleasant individual. On that point she and Rory were in total agreement.

Dismissing Rory from her mind, Stella concentrated on the road ahead. The weather was milder in this part of the world. Although it was too early for tourists, soon the roads would be clogged with caravans and surfers eager to ride the waves. Stella loved the holiday season. The visitors brought vibrancy to the community and injected capital into local businesses. Hikers tramped the moors and visitors of a more romantic persuasion lapped up the stories of smugglers and ship-wrecks.

Stella smiled. No way could she class herself as a starry-eyed romantic, but as a child she had loved the legends associated with this part of the world and many an afternoon she would venture onto the windswept moors in search of adventure. Nothing too disastrous had happened to her, and after a day's fresh air she would return home ready for one of Amy's cream teas.

She parked her car at the top of the hill that led down to the village. An arrangement with the golf club allowed residents to use their facilities on payment of a small fee.

Fisherman's Rest Cottage was at the end of a terrace. Slipping her hand through the letterbox, Stella retrieved the key that dangled on a piece of string inside. She couldn't count the number of times she'd cautioned Amy against this practice.

'Anyone could gain access to the cottage,' she said.

'They're welcome to anything of value they can find,' Amy would respond. 'My family are the only valuables in my life.'

Stella found a handwritten note by the kitchen kettle: *Scones, jam and cream in the fridge. Help yourself.* Amy had signed off with a dozen kisses.

Stella did justice to the scones and a mug of tea before going upstairs to check on her bedroom.

Amy's voice dragged Stella from the depths of a deep sleep. 'I thought we'd had one of those break-ins you're always warning me about.'

'W . . . what?' Stella asked, blinking up at her.

'All that was left of the scones was a plate of crumbs, and like that fairy tale, I found someone sleeping in your bed.'

Stella scrambled upright, stifling a yawn. 'What's the time?'

'Half past eight. Your grandfather's gone for fish and chips.' Amy held out her arms. 'Give us a kiss.'

Stella inhaled the familiar smell of stained wood and varnish that she always associated with her grand-parents.

'You've lost weight,' Amy accused Stella. 'That wretched Mark Dashwood, I suppose?' The astute eyes narrowed. 'Or is there a new man in your life now?'

'I haven't got time for men,' Stella insisted.

'Excellent.' Amy beamed at her. 'It can be a long wait to find the right one, but when you do, make sure it's someone I like. I never took to Mark, but as he's history we won't waste time talking about him. Now, make yourself presentable, then come downstairs.'

A glass of cool white wine was ready for her on the patio. 'I've turned on the heaters,' Amy told her.

Jim kissed Stella, then Amy passed over a wrapped parcel of newspaper. Freshly caught cod and golden chips had never tasted better, Stella thought as they ate in companionable silence. When they'd finished, Amy rolled up her greaseproof paper into a ball and lobbed it into the wastepaper bin.

Jim raised his eyebrows in mock exasperation. 'I regret your grandmother has not acquired any gracious table manners since you last saw her.'

'Good food in your stomach is more important than using the right knife and fork,' Amy retaliated. 'Who's for walnut gâteau?'

'I don't think I've got the room,' Stella protested.

'Nonsense, you're on holiday.'

'I'll get it.' Jim rose to his feet.

Looking over her shoulder to make sure her grandfather was well out of earshot, Stella leaned forward. 'You said you had something to tell me,' she whispered.

Amy paused. 'We're moving.'

'But you've been here for years.'

'It's time for a change, so we're off to live in Spain.'

8

'Where in Spain are you going?' Stella asked.

'Cádiz. It's very like Clovelly.'

'In what way?' Stella demanded, unable to see any resemblance.

'We have cream and they have sherry,' Amy laughed.

'That's not much to go on.'

'They have fish markets where they sell the day's catch. It's full of tiny back streets that are a treasure to explore. We share ancestry too. There's many a Spaniard who stayed on here after being shipwrecked off the coast in the Middle Ages,' Amy explained, warming to her theme, 'and I'm taking a crash course in Spanish.'

Stella recalled a school history lesson. 'Didn't Sir Francis Drake upset the locals by attacking Cádiz?'

'I hope they've forgiven us for that

transgression. Cádiz is surrounded by water, so Jim wouldn't miss his beloved sea, and there's plenty happening on the Atlantic coast. If he should get homesick, Gibraltar's not far away, so we can pop over the border any time we fancy.'

⋆　⋆　⋆

When Jim had returned to the patio with their coffee the previous evening, Amy had hastily hushed Stella. Now she and Stella were walking barefoot along the beach with wet sand oozing between their toes.

'Jenny persuaded me to go for it,' Amy confessed. 'Another thing — she's pregnant.'

'Why didn't you tell me?'

'She didn't want to make it public. The first few months were traumatic. Her blood pressure was high but everything's fine now. We're hoping for a girl. My boys have produced sons, so we're over-manned, you could say. The thing is, she's on her own. She and Max haven't split up,' Amy hastened to add. 'He's been offered a crewing job. It's for six weeks, and during the quiet season; it's good money but he doesn't want to leave Jenny on her own.'

Two years ago, Amy's daughter had split from her partner of many years because marriage wasn't his scene. To cheer herself up Jenny had embarked on a European tour. Her travels had taken her no further than Andalusia. Within two months she had met Max, and within another two months they were married.

'Couldn't you go out there for an extended visit?'

'Jim suggested we move there permanently.'

'Granddad? He doesn't speak Spanish. He hates golf, and what would he do all day?'

'He could learn Spanish, and there is plenty to do.'

'Putting up sheds?'

'Working in the boatyards. His skills

wouldn't go to waste.'

'What's going to happen to the business?'

Amy tossed a pebble into the sea and watched it skim across the diamond-bright water.

'We had another stroke of luck. A young couple came down from London for a weekend break. The lady fell in love with Jim's carvings. You know those little animals he whittles from leftover bits of wood? She bought one and we got talking. I was horrified to learn they spent twelve hours every day staring at a screen. I told them they should get a life. That was when they confided that their dream was to move down here, and before I knew it we'd struck a deal.'

'You've already sold up?'

'As good as. I kept telling Jim you had to know what was going on. It's been a weight on my mind.'

'When do you intend leaving?'

'Not yet. We're letting out Fisher-man's Cottage. I've appointed an agent,

Mr Skinner. You went to college with his daughter.'

Stella wriggled her toes in the sand. 'Do you really have to go?'

'I hoped you would be happy for us.'

'I know I'm being selfish, but you've always been here for me.'

'And we always will,' Amy assured her. 'Spain is only a couple of hours away by air.' She touched Stella's arm. 'If you really can't take to the idea, we'll back out.'

'I wouldn't hear of it. And I'll be out there like a shot the minute the baby's born.'

'You don't know how much it means to me to have your blessing. Now it's your turn,' Amy insisted.

'For what?'

'You can tell me what's wrong for a start.'

'I've lost my job.'

'You're freelance, aren't you?'

'I moved in with a lovely lady as her companion. It was a good arrangement. I carried on with my work during the day, then we had dinner together in the evenings.'

'Has she got a family?'

'That's the problem.' Stella briefly updated Amy on all that had happened. When she finished the older woman burst out laughing.

'You've done exactly the right thing, my girl.'

'By getting myself dismissed?'

'By getting this son of hers to do all the donkey work. What a pompous ass. You wait, he'll come crawling back.'

'I don't think Rory Loates does crawl.'

'Rory Loates?' Amy raised her eyebrows.

Stella's reply was a curt, 'Yes.'

'I never miss his interviews.'

'I think I might have put one of them in jeopardy,' Stella confessed. 'He was due to meet someone important the day I left. I didn't hang around after the power went off. I don't think he got to London.'

'I could have warned him not to mess

with you.' Amy laughed. 'I tried it once or twice when you were going through a difficult phase. It was an experience I lived to regret.'

'I was never difficult,' Stella protested.

'No more than the average teenager I suppose, but you could disrupt the household for a week.' Amy squeezed her hand. 'Well, good luck. I confidently predict when you check your mobile there'll be a message begging you to come back.'

'I wouldn't count on it.'

'Meanwhile, I expect poor old Jim is worried about us. He'll be thinking you've talked me into staying on here.'

'He's really that keen to go?' Stella asked.

'He feels it's now or never.'

A sharp breeze blew in off the sea.

'The tide is about to turn.' Amy shaded her eyes out to the horizon. 'We'd better take the cliff path.'

By the time they reached the cottage fine rain had soaked their outer clothes.

Jim poked an anxious head around the sitting-room door.

'Put the kettle on, would you, while I take a shower?' Amy asked him.

Jim perched on an armrest after she left the room. 'Amy's told you?'

'Yes.' Stella nodded.

'I've always been an emotional coward. My generation were more buttoned up than today's youngsters.'

'I must say, Granddad, I never thought of you as a sundowner.'

'That's something I'll never be,' Jim insisted. 'An acquaintance of mine runs a boat builders' yard out there and he's promised me some work. Amy will be busy looking after Jennifer and the baby, and she can always help out in the yard. She's as good as any man at weatherproofing.'

'Looks like it's winners all round,' Stella finished off for him.

'You're sure you don't mind?'

'I'll miss you, but it will be nice to have a ready-made holiday destination.'

Padded footsteps along the landing

alerted them to the fact that Amy had finished her shower.

'Best get the tea on.' Jim leapt to his feet.

Leaning back in her chair, Stella retrieved her mobile from her handbag. Amy was right. There were several missed messages, and they were all from Rory Loates.

9

Both Jim and Amy were up to see Stella off after a breakfast of coffee and toast.

'Do you have everything?' Amy demanded as they walked up the hill to the golf club. 'You can reheat the casserole for dinner tonight.'

'I don't know what sort of reception I'm going to get and whether I'll be welcome to dinner.'

Amy kissed her on the cheek. 'Ring to let us know you've arrived safely.'

'And drive carefully,' Jim added, hugging his granddaughter.

It was a cool, crisp morning and Stella made good time. She pulled over into a lay-by and ate Amy's crab sandwiches. The midday sun was warm and she put her head back and closed her eyes. A car starting up jolted her awake, and after taking a few moments to stretch her legs and deposit her litter in the bin Stella recommenced her journey.

There was now more traffic on the road and progress was slow. Several sets of road works added to the delay, and it was with relief Stella turned off for Knight's Walk. She drove round the back of Minster House and into the courtyard. Sparky raced out to greet her, followed by Rory, who yanked open the driver's door and demanded to know where she had been.

'Good evening,' she greeted him coolly. 'I trust your mother and the children are well.'

'Come and give me a kiss,' a voice called from the kitchen.

With Sparky snapping at her heels, Stella waved at Pamela, who was standing in the doorway with the aid of two sticks.

'Sit down,' Stella urged her. 'You know the doctor doesn't like you putting weight on that ankle.'

'Thank goodness you're back.' Pamela accepted Stella's offer of an arm to lean on and they shuffled towards a kitchen chair. 'The children were impossible when they discovered you'd gone. They're back at school now until Friday. I could strangle that son of mine. When I found out what he'd done I gave him a piece of my mind.' She swept a hand around the kitchen. 'Look at the mess. He's flooded the floor. The lights have been on and off constantly, and I've missed goodness knows how many hospital appointments. Is it any wonder my ankle's not healing?'

Pamela glared over her shoulder as there was a movement behind Stella. 'Have you apologised to Stella?' she demanded as Rory carried Amy's casserole into the kitchen.

'I found this on the back seat,' he said. 'It smells fantastic.'

Pamela's eyes lit up. 'I'll heat it up.'

'You'll do no such thing,' Stella insisted.

After a brief squabble during which, she later recalled, Rory never did get round to apologising to her, the casserole was placed in the oven.

'Don't forget to switch it on,' Pamela instructed him.

'I only forgot once,' Rory replied in a tight voice.

'All we had to eat for dinner that night was toast and jam,' Pamela grumbled.

Rory cleared a space on the table for Amy's scones, which were demolished with unseemly haste. While the fragrant smell of sage and onion pervaded the kitchen, Stella called Amy to let her know she was back and that she would be staying at Minster House for the time being.

'Told you so,' was Amy's smug response.

After supper Pamela opted for an early night. 'If I come down in the morning to find Stella's gone again, then you're no son of mine,' she threatened Rory.

'Would you like a glass of wine?' Rory offered after Pamela had gone upstairs.

He came back with a tray and nibbles. 'I found these in your grandmother's bag of goodies.' He indicated a plate of savoury biscuits.

'You can't still be hungry.'

Rory swallowed a mouthful of cheese puffs. 'I had no idea running a house was so challenging, especially with two adolescents and a fractious mother in tow.'

'Your mother's not fractious,' Stella protested.

'She is when the lights go out for the third time in the middle of her favourite soap. Anyway,' he added after sipping some wine, 'can we put the past behind us? I've had a rethink.'

'And?' Stella prompted.

'There are several things I can do from home, so I'll be around more. But regarding the running of the house — it's all yours.'

'The agreement was that I should be a companion to your mother, not a housekeeper,' Stella objected.

'You're not thinking of leaving?'

'I'd hate to be the cause of an estrangement between you and your mother, but I have a demanding job too.'

'The children have promised to look after their rooms and help as much as they can. Mrs Watts has agreed to put in extra hours. I'll arrange an allowance for you.'

'That won't be necessary,' replied Stella. 'I'm living here rent-free.'

'You don't have to touch it if you don't want to, but think of it as an emergency backup.'

They lapsed into silence for a few moments.

'Have you received any more unpleasant voice mails?' Rory asked eventually. 'I can help there too.'

Stella shook her head.

'Can you tell me what started things off?' Rory asked.

'I took some photos,' Stella admitted, 'and I inadvertently snapped two men in the background. One of them didn't like it. He was the one demanding all the copies.'

'May I see the print?'

'In all the confusion I've misplaced it,' Stella admitted.

'Can you describe the men?'

'One was wearing a camel-hair coat and sporting a flamboyant buttonhole. He was standing next to a man in a warehouse coat. A package was exchanging hands.'

'Sounds like a payoff.' Rory frowned. 'Where were you?'

'At a gallery. I was there to photograph works of art for insurance purposes.'

'I'll get it.' Rory went to answer the telephone.

After a murmured exchange he came back into the sitting room. 'Fenella wants to have a word with you.'

'Stella?' Fenella asked when she answered the phone. 'You *are* staying, aren't you? I mean I love Nan to bits, and Tom's OK as brothers go, but he's, like, so irritating. Did you know Rory's got me a new hairdryer? If I promise not to fuse the lights again, you *will* stay, won't you?' she pleaded.

'Ground rules?' Stella insisted.

'Absolutely,' Fenella agreed. 'Tom says to tell you he'll keep his room tidy and clear up after breakfast.'

'In that case,' Stella relented, 'I'll stay.'

Her remark was met with an ear-deafening whoop of joy. 'See you on Friday. Pick us up as soon as you can after half past three.'

Before Stella could object, Fenella rang off. There was no sign of Rory in the sitting room, so she made her way across to the cow byre. Opening a few windows, she let in some cool evening air. Then, following Pamela's example, she had an early night.

★　★　★

A boiler-suited Rory knocked on her door the next evening. 'I need to test the oil pressure. Want to come for a spin?'

He'd spent most of the day tinkering with his vintage car. Every so often the silence was punctured by a vigorous application of the engine and several mini-explosions as blockages were cleared.

'You've been cooped up all day. I've got you some goggles,' he said, holding up an oily pair of eye protectors. 'Have you got a hat?'

'Are we going to a wedding?'

Rory grinned. 'I'm not suggesting a garden party affair, just something to ram on your head. It gets pretty draughty once I get up speed. Five minutes?'

Stella donned the goggles, shrugged on an old anorak, and rammed a woolly hat on her head before joining him in the forecourt.

'The door catch sticks. You'll have to jump in.'

Stella shoehorned herself into a cramped seating space, doing her best to avoid the pools of oil in the footwell.

'Settled? Hang on to your hat,' Rory bellowed. With a lurch to the left he swung the car towards the gates and down the access road leading to Knight's Walk.

Tendrils of hedge swiped the sides of the car as the lane narrowed to single-track. Every so often startled sheep scurried for cover as the roaring beast made its way past the field. Stella wrinkled her nose, unable to ignore the smell of burning oil. She nudged Rory and pointed to the falling needle on the pressure gauge. He nodded and lunged for a grassy bank before grinding to a halt.

'You're going to have to get out,' Rory announced. 'You're sitting on the tool box.'

Stella squatted on the verge and watched Rory lift the bonnet. 'Could you pass me a wrench? Not that one. The bigger one.'

Without bothering to thank her, he returned his attention to the intricacies of the engine. There had been some talk about a visit to a thatched barn for refreshment. Stella's hopes faded at the sound of running liquid. 'Something's leaking,' she volunteered.

'It's raining. Quick, cover the seats.'

Stella was struggling with a filthy tarpaulin. 'Are you going to be much longer?'

'A few minutes.'

Rory's teeth gleamed white from his oily face. Stella leaned against the tarpaulin, wondering if he would object if she were to snuggle under it for warmth.

'There,' he said a few moments later, 'that should do the trick. Ready?'

'Where are we going now?'

'For that drink.'

'We can't be seen in public like this,' Stella protested in horror, looking down at her oily hands and feet.

'Why not?' Rory sounded genuinely surprised. 'Old cars are great icebreakers. People are always eager to take a look and ask questions, you see.'

His face was full of amusement as Stella clambered over the door and landed in her seat with an unladylike thump. 'Having fun?' he asked.

'I look an absolute sight.' Stella scrubbed at her face with a tissue.

Rory tugged at a recalcitrant curl that had escaped her bobble hat. 'Your nose is red,' he admitted, 'and there's a huge smear of oil on your cheek, but I shouldn't let it worry you. Are you ready to roll?'

After a couple of false starts the car coughed into life. It had stopped raining. The air smelt green and fresh. They moved forward. Stella no longer felt cold. With a wry smile, she admitted, 'I'm having a wonderful time.'

10

Mr Jenkins greeted Stella with a friendly smile as she parked at the back of the art gallery. 'I was beginning to wonder what had happened to you.'

'I've been rather busy,' Stella explained, getting out of her car.

'We've been hectic too. There's an art scam doing the rounds. I've given instructions for my staff to double-check everything and if they suspect anything untoward then they are to report back to me. I can vouch for my regulars, but temps are here today and gone tomorrow. There are some very dishonest people about, and they'll do anything for extra money.' He tutted. 'Anyway, come on in.'

He led her through the workshop to a makeshift office. 'Sorry about the mess. We have been pushed for space with this valuation.'

Stella squashed into a corner of the desk, then retrieved her portfolio from her case.

Mr Jenkins finished his inspection. 'Very good spec. I appreciate it was a rush job. If you send in your invoice we'll settle immediately.'

'You mentioned a scam?' Stella queried.

'You should know the details,' Mr Jenkins began, 'in case you are commissioned by another gallery. I mentioned to you that we undertake to clean works of art?'

Stella nodded.

'In a place like this it's not easy to keep track of everyone. Visitors sign in and out, but you've seen some of the squiggles in the signature book. A competent handwriting expert wouldn't be able to decipher them.'

'Have you been a victim of this scam?' Stella asked.

'I couldn't say for certain. I am meticulous about record-keeping, but if someone puts their mind to it, there is nothing to stop them passing artwork details to an outsider.'

'Then what happens?' Stella asked.

'This is only my theory, you understand.'

Stella nodded.

'Someone takes down the details, a copy is made, the original is returned to the owner, and the copy is sold.'

Stella was beginning to wonder if the scene she had photographed was a payoff. It could have been an innocent meeting between two people. However, no one had ever threatened her before.

'Can you see yourself out?' Mr Jenkins shook Stella's hand.

Stella heaved her bag over her shoulder. As she approached her car, she noticed the passenger door wasn't closed. As she opened it wider, some loose papers floated to the ground. The glove compartment gaped open. One of the loaders emerged from a shed carrying a tray of mugs.

'You didn't see anyone hanging around my car, did you?' she asked him.

'Can't say I did. Is there a problem?'

'No,' Stella assured him quickly. 'Thanks.'

She jumped into the driver's seat. There was no damage done and she didn't want to be delayed. She had promised Pamela she would collect Fenella and Tom.

If she had been expecting a rapturous welcome from June's children, Stella would have been disappointed. Fenella was slouching against a tree trunk. She slumped into the passenger seat without a word and carried on texting.

'Where's Tom?' Stella demanded.

'No idea.' Fenella didn't raise her eyes from her touch screen.

Stella accosted a passing pupil. 'Where might I find Tom Waugh?'

'Down at the nets.'

Stella strode down to the pavilion.

'Stella.' Tom waved his bat at her.

'Have you any idea of the time?' She tapped her watch.

'Not when he's batting he hasn't,' the bowler advised her with a cheerful smile.

'You couldn't get my things and take them to the car, could you? Please?' Tom wheedled.

Stella relented, unable to face a scene. 'Twenty minutes, no longer.'

Tom had already turned away and was busy wielding his bat, preparing for another hit.

'Where've you been?' Fenella demanded when she got back to the car.

'Take this,' Stella replied through gritted teeth.

'It's Tom's stuff,' she objected.

Tom chose that moment to race towards them from the direction of the nets. 'Got held up,' he explained, not looking in the least repentant as Stella thrust his case at him. 'Did you pack my cricket manual?'

'I have no idea,' Stella replied, 'and I have no intention of going back for it. Now get in.'

The half-hour journey home was completed in near silence. Fenella's fingers tapped out more messages and Tom, engrossed in heavy metal downloads, only opened his eyes as they drove through the gates of Minster House. He was out of the rear passenger door before Stella had brought the car fully to a halt.

'Tom,' she bellowed in a voice that would have done credit to a sergeant major on a drill ground, 'get back here immediately.'

'There's no need to shout,' he grumbled.

'You will pick up your bag and take it to your room. I refuse to run round after you.'

'Stella . . . ' he began.

'I mean it.'

'All right,' he said with a breezy smile. He slammed the car door shut and ran towards the kitchen door with Sparky barking around his ankles.

'Fenella?' Stella nudged the girl. 'We're home,' she said.

'You are staying this time, aren't you?' she asked in a small voice.

Restraining herself from putting out a hand to stroke the girl's untidy hair, Stella reassured her. 'Of course.'

Without a further word Fenella turned away, and yanking open her door slouched after Tom.

* * *

'We could go to the activity centre tomorrow,' Rory suggested over supper.

Pamela, tired from her hospital visit, had opted for scrambled eggs on toast in her bedroom.

'That way Nan could have a quiet rest.' Rory looked at Fenella.

'If we're a nuisance you only have to say,' she replied with a sulky look on her face.

Rory cast a look of exasperation at Stella.

'I'll serve up,' Stella offered. 'Tom, come and help me.'

'Is anything wrong?' Rory asked his niece as the other two left the table.

'Nothing,' she muttered.

Over in the kitchen, while Stella warmed the plates, Tom confided, 'She's been seriously weird.'

'In what way?' Stella asked.

'She won't talk to me at school — not that I care, but she's mixing with a horrible bunch of girls. Gruesome Gloria is the ringleader and she's always in trouble. Can I eat mine in my room?'

Tom grabbed his plate of lasagne and was out of the kitchen before Stella could protest or ask further questions.

'I'm not staying here either.' Fenella followed his example.

'So much for a cosy family meal,' Rory sighed. 'You're not going to desert me too, are you?' he asked Stella.

'I've only got stale bread and cheese in my fridge.'

'In that case I'll get us something to drink and we can catch up on our day.'

Rory frowned when Stella updated him on what Tom had told her. 'I don't like the sound of it. Fenella's at a vulnerable age, and with her parents away there's no one she can turn to if she's in trouble.'

'There's your mother.'

Rory shook his head. 'She's two generations away from today's problems, if you know what I mean.' He looked hopefully at Stella.

'I don't think she would listen to anything I have to say,' Stella replied.

'There's only an eight-year age gap between you,' Rory pointed out.

'To someone of Fenella's age, that's a generation.'

'Didn't you have problems when you were growing up?'

Stella twirled her fork around the rapidly cooling cheese sauce on her plate. Amy had borne the brunt of Stella's uncertainties and night after night sat up with her, assuring her she was loved and beautiful and saying all the right things until they both eventually emerged from the trauma, drained but still friends.

'I'll try to have a word with her,' Stella replied. 'Perhaps I could find some time tomorrow if you could persuade her and Tom to come to the activities centre.'

'I'm not sure now it was such a good idea.'

'A change of scenery will do us all good,' Stella assured him.

Rory put a hand across the table and touched hers. 'Thanks.'

The heat of the kitchen, combined with the food and wine, brought a deep blush to Stella's complexion. Her feelings for Rory were in a jumble. Since her return from Devon he had done everything he could, from rearranging his business life to making sure he was available to help with his mother's requirements. Previously she'd thought of him as an opinionated macho male, but she now saw a caring man who was doing his best to hold the fractured family together.

'It wasn't what you bargained for, was it?' Rory asked. 'The family from hell?'

'All families have trying times. That's what life is about. But you pull through together.'

'And Fenella?'

'She'll be all right,' Stella assured him.

'If you can't get through you could try ducking her in the water trough on the roller coaster ride.' Rory smiled.

'That would be an experience I might live to regret,' Stella replied.

'Only a suggestion. I'll be there for you if things turn difficult,' he promised. 'Only, I don't know if men are much good in these types of situations. Do you think I should contact June?'

'Let's see what it's all about first,' Stella suggested. 'We may be making a fuss about nothing.'

Rory blinked at the bottle of wine. 'We've finished it.'

Stella hid a yawn behind the back of her hand. 'Sorry, it's past my bedtime.'

'I'll see to things here if you want to get to bed.'

Stella stretched out her legs. Rory leaned in towards her but a sharp bark from Sparky interrupted them. Stella straightened up in shock as the cold realisation of the situation hit her. Rory

106

had been about to kiss her — and what was worse, she wouldn't have objected.

'Someone wants a walk,' she backed off. 'I'll see you in the morning.'

She fled from the warmth of the kitchen, welcoming the feel of the cool night air on her face.

11

The theme park was proving a success. After raising her eyes in teenage boredom at some of the activities on offer, Fenella threw herself into the water ride with enthusiasm, shrieking with delight when Stella got soaked.

Passing on the mud match, Stella watched Tom win a prize in his category. Although he was wearing protective clothing, she suspected some mud would have seeped through to his shirt and trousers. Hoping the washing machine was up to the task, she joined Fenella in a junior quad bike race. When they came last in their category Stella feared a tantrum from her co-driver, but after they collided with a bale of hay, all she'd done was laugh and pull straw out of her hair.

'That was terrific,' she enthused. 'Let's get a toffee apple.'

Stella and Fenella stood by the kiosk,

crunching on the sticky coating covering the soft flesh of the apple. Every so often the public address system announced various activities, causing swarms of youngsters to tug reluctant parents off for yet another physical experience. In the background a barrel organ churned out constant music. The air smelt of onions and hot coffee.

'We'd better find the boys.' Stella disposed of her toffee apple stick in the rubbish bin.

'Not yet,' Fenella protested, and put out a hand to clutch Stella's. Her skin felt soft and warm and trusting.

Recognising that this might be the moment for their quiet word, Stella asked, 'Fancy a soft drink to rinse the toffee out of our teeth?'

Clutching milkshakes, they perched on wobbly seats around an equally wobbly plastic table.

'Enjoying yourself?' Stella asked.

Fenella slurped some milk through her straw. She shrugged. Stella took a deep breath. 'You've a lucky girl, you know,' she began.

'Your mother didn't go off and leave you.' The light of challenge darkened Fenella's brown eyes.

'Your mother loves you very much, Fenella, and so does your father.' Stella held up a hand to stem any interruption. 'They're working hard to keep the family together. That's why your grandmother and Rory are looking after you and Tom.'

There was another slurpy noise as Fenella sucked on her straw. 'Did you talk to your mother about things when you were my age?' she asked.

'I talked to my step-grandmother,' Stella replied. 'She and my grandfather brought me up after my parents died.'

From the way Fenella widened her eyes, Stella had the feeling this revelation about her personal circumstances changed the young girl's perception of her. Stella seized her chance. 'If you've got anything you'd like to talk about, I'm ready to listen. Is everything all right at school?'

'It's cool,' Fenella insisted.

Stella nodded. To probe further might undo the tentative progress they had made. 'Good. Well, don't forget my offer, I'm always available.'

'You went away. You left us.' The confrontation was back in Fenella's eyes.

'That won't happen again.'

'Do you promise?'

Stella hesitated, not wanting to give her word then not keep it. 'I promise that I'll always be available to talk to you,' she said.

Fenella was quick to pick up on Stella's hesitation. 'Does that mean you're going away again?'

'I won't make false promises, Fenella. I am not a member of your family, and should your grandmother have plans for the extension then I would probably have to move.'

'She hasn't, and I know she likes you. She said so.'

'I like her too. So let's have no more talk about leaving. I'll give you my social media contacts. That way I'll always be available.'

'Brilliant,' Fenella mumbled, doing her best not to look grateful.

'How would you like a day out just, the two of us?' Stella proposed. 'We could get nail art done, or do a beauty salon.'

'Hair extensions?'

'If you want.'

Fenella was now pink with excitement.

'I'll arrange something,' Stella said.

'What's that you're drinking?' Tom asked as he descended on them, Rory in tow, whilst eyeing their empty tumblers suspiciously.

'Milkshakes, and there's none left for you,' Fenella replied.

'We've had toffee apples too,' Stella informed Rory before Fenella confessed all.

'Why didn't I get one of those either?' Tom demanded.

'Because you weren't here,' Fenella replied. 'Anyway, Stella and I were talking and we didn't want brothers interfering. We've arranged a day out. Boys are not welcome.'

'Girl stuff?' A look of horror crossed Tom's face.

'Yes.'

'Count me out,' he said with a shudder. 'I'm hungry,' he announced.

'Come on,' said Rory, who had been hovering behind Tom. He tugged at Tom's jacket. 'As the girls left us out, let's get something to eat.' Over Tom's head and behind Fenella's back, Rory raised his eyebrows in a brief gesture of enquiry. Stella gave him a brief nod.

Tom began reading from the programme. 'There's an archery contest at two o'clock. Can we have a go, Rory?' He unwrapped a chocolate biscuit.

'I'd like to have a go too.' Fenella picked up the second chocolate biscuit on the plate and began nibbling at the cream coating.

'Do you feel like playing Maid Marian to my Robin Hood?' Rory asked Stella. 'Or shall we go girls against boys?'

'Fen and I could beat you two oldies any day,' Tom boasted.

'Tom,' Rory reprimanded his nephew, 'that wasn't a very polite thing to say.'

'Sorry,' he mumbled.

'I wouldn't be too sure you'd win anyway,' Stella retaliated. 'Archery is like photography. You need a steady hand for both.'

'Girls against boys it is then,' Fenella announced.

'You're on.' Tom snatched up the last sandwich, beating Fenella by a hair's breadth.

'I wanted that,' she objected.

'Too late, and you've already scoffed a toffee apple and a chocolate biscuit,' Tom said before cramming the sandwich into his mouth.

'Not to mention a milkshake with marshmallows,' Rory added.

'Would you like something grown-up to eat?' Rory asked Stella. 'They do salads and quiche at the bar.'

'Yuck.' Tom wiped his mouth with the back of his hand. 'Rabbit food.'

'This coffee will do me fine,' Stella replied.

'Well I'm having a pasty,' Rory said.

He came back with another loaded tray, and despite her protestations Stella tucked into a small portion of quiche and lettuce.

'Hands off,' Rory commanded as Tom grabbed a chip from his plate. 'You've had yours.'

'It's the fresh air making me hungry,' he explained.

'Everything makes you hungry,' Fenella said.

'Why are you looking at your nails in that funny way?' Tom demanded.

'I was wondering what little stars would look like.'

Tom crossed his eyes and made a whirling gesture with his hand. 'Stupid or what?'

'I'm talking about nail art, goofo,' Fenella said.

'I never know what you're talking about.'

A lively debate ensued between the pair of them.

'You've worked wonders,' Rory murmured out the side of his mouth. 'They are actually behaving like a normal brother and sister.' He paused. 'By the way, I have a suggestion.'

'Yes?' Stella asked guardedly.

'It might be a good idea if you moved into the main part of the house to sleep.'

'There isn't room.'

'We could swap.'

'Why?'

'I think Fenella would value it. Tom too.'

'What about my work? I use the study and everything's laid out.'

'You can still keep that on. All I need is a bed and somewhere to store some of my things. I don't suppose I'll be there much of the time.'

'What are you two talking about?' Fenella demanded suspiciously.

'Stella's going to move into Rory's bedroom,' Tom replied, adding, 'I overheard.'

'What?' Fenella squeaked.

'Rory wants to move into the extension,' Stella quickly explained, 'if you're agreeable to the idea.'

'I don't mind.' Fenella gave a casual

shrug, but Stella glimpsed the chink in her armour and that secretly she liked the arrangement.

Stella suggested a face-saver. 'That way you could share my hairdryer.'

'Rory bought me a new one,' Fenella said, then added, 'But thanks for the offer, and I'd quite like you to have the room next to mine.'

'*I'm* in the room next to you,' Tom protested.

'You can move into Rory's room.'

'S'pose I can.' Tom began fidgeting now he had finished eating.

'It's all settled then.' Rory smiled round at everyone. 'If there are no further objections, I declare this meeting closed.'

'If we don't hurry up,' Stella said, clapping her hands to make her voice heard above Tom's and Fenella's as they began to make plans about the room changes, 'no one will get a chance to move anywhere. Are we still on for the archery contest?'

'Rory,' a smoky voice purred. An

elegant female stood behind him. 'Long time no see,' she said with a smile that reminded Stella of a cat hovering over a dish of cream.

'Jackie.' Rory stood up.

Putting out an elegantly manicured hand, she held onto his arm as if to stop him moving away from her. 'Out with the family, are you?' Her green eyes swept over Stella.

'I don't think you've met Tom and Fenella,' Rory said.

Tom chose that moment to suck on his straw. The bubbling noise drowned Jackie's reply and earned him a frown of reproof from Stella.

'And this is Stella.'

Jackie now began to stroke Rory's arm, not bothering to look at Stella. 'Perhaps we could have a drink? We've loads to catch up on.'

'I can't.' Rory softened his refusal with a smile that didn't quite reach his eyes.

'I'm sure Stephanie could look after the children.'

'Her name's Stella, and I'm not a child,' Fenella butted in.

'Neither am I,' Tom added for good measure.

There was no warmth in Jackie's eyes as her look now encompassed the little party sitting around the plastic table. 'Another time, perhaps,' she suggested to Rory. 'When you're less busy.'

'We'll see,' he replied.

'You still have my number?'

Tom began rocking backwards and forwards on his wobbly seat. Fearing an accident, Stella stood up. 'You can catch up with us later, Rory. We'll be over by the archery tent.'

'We're going to take part in the contest,' Fenella explained.

'How very enthusiastic of you,' Jackie drawled, raising a plucked eyebrow.

'Stella's got a steady hand,' Fenella said as she linked an arm through Stella's.

'I'm sure she has.' Jackie's expression was now glacial and left Stella with the uneasy suspicion that she thought she was aiming her arrows at Rory.

The public address system spluttered into life. 'For those of you who haven't yet registered for the archery contest, please do so now.'

Tom tugged at Stella's free hand. 'Hurry up.'

'What about Rory?' Fenella looked over her shoulder.

'Coming,' he called after them. 'Lovely to see you again, Jackie. Give my regards to Mike.'

'Didn't I tell you that's all over?' she called after him.

'She is so obvious,' Fenella hissed in Stella's ear.

'Whatever she is doing is none of our business,' Stella responded firmly.

'She hates you.'

'She doesn't know me.'

'She thinks you and Rory are an item. If I were you I should look out.'

'Why?'

'She'll nab him from under your nose.'

'Then she's welcome to him.'

Rory caught them up. 'Who's welcome to what?'

'Stella says Jackie's welcome to you.'

Flames of embarrassment coloured Stella's face. 'That's not what I said at all,' she protested.

'In that case, would you mind very much if I held your other hand?' Rory enquired, a quirky smile curving the corner of his mouth.

'Of course Stella wouldn't mind,' Fenella giggled. 'Are you trying to make Jackie jealous?'

'I'm trying to get her off my back, and it would do my cause no harm if she thought Stella and I were involved.'

Without waiting for her assent, Rory linked his fingers through Stella's. Fenella squeezed her other hand in a gesture of complicity and did a little dance on the grass. 'This is fun,' she announced.

'You lot haven't got time to hold hands,' Tom said, pushing everyone forwards. 'The archery registration is about to close.'

Fenella cast a glance over her shoulder to where Jackie was still standing by their abandoned table. 'Nice to meet you,' Fenella called over with a cheery wave.

Rory rolled his eyes. 'I owe you one,' he mouthed at Stella.

'I'm not sure having a quiet word with your niece was such a good idea,' Stella whispered back as Fenella let go of her hand and raced after Tom. 'She's getting all sorts of ideas about us.'

'Playing Cupid, is she?' Rory grinned.

'You're not taking this seriously.' Stella snatched her hand away from his. 'There's no need to keep up the subterfuge. Jackie's gone.'

'Pity,' Rory said with a shrug. 'I was rather enjoying myself.'

'Let's get one thing straight.'

Rory widened his eyes. 'My, you are looking fierce, Stella. Go on, the floor's yours.'

'There is not, nor will there ever be, anything of a romantic nature between us.'

'I wasn't thinking of a romance,' Rory protested.

'In that case, you won't be disappointed.' Stella held up a hand. 'Now, Tom seems to have enrolled us in this archery contest.' He was running towards them, flapping two forms in the air. 'I don't know about you, but I shall enjoy getting a bull's eye.'

'As long as I'm not the target.'

Tom was breathing heavily from the effort of running across the field. He dragged at Rory's hand. 'Stella, you have to go over there.'

The next moment Fenella was bundling her into a high-visibility jacket and thrusting equipment at her. 'We've got to show we're better than the boys,' she said. 'Ready?'

Stella trudged after the girl, her feet making squishy noises as they sank into the grass.

12

'Greetings from Cádiz — well just outside, but I can't pronounce the name of our village. It's all zeds and you have to lisp. Plays havoc with the teeth. When are you coming to visit?'

Stella sauntered into the sunshine to take Amy's call. 'How's Jennifer?' she asked.

'Blossoming. Sends you her love.'

'And Granddad?'

'Up to his armpits in boat parts. He comes home every night smelling of wood and paint thinner, so no change there then.' Amy's guffaw was ear-splitting. 'So how are tricks?'

'We've sorted out our differences and I'm sleeping in the house now.'

'You've been evicted from the cow shed?' Amy chuckled. 'Weren't you milking the girls fast enough?'

'Pamela's son is living there.'

Her remark was greeted with a long silence. 'Is this the same son who was the cause of your trouble?'

'Sort of,' Stella hedged.

'I recognise that tone of voice. You want me to butt out.'

'I don't want you matchmaking,' Stella insisted.

'Would I?'

'Yes.'

'I want to see you settled and happy. After that business with Mark Dashwood, you deserve some luck. Now, when I've got to grips with the new computer I'll be online, video links at the ready. Meanwhile, you've got the number here, haven't you? And if you fancy some sun the fares are on me, so don't do cheap.'

Stella hung up with a smile on her face just as the main house telephone rang. She answered the call in the kitchen.

'Is Rory there?'

Stella's heart sank. 'He's at work.'

'It's Jackie James.' This was the third

call in as many days. 'Are you sure you're passing on my messages?'

Stella tried to explain she had pinned them to the corkboard, but Jackie wasn't listening to explanations.

'Do you have a location number I could call?'

'Only in an emergency.'

'This is an emergency of sorts.'

'I am referring to family emergencies.' Stella did her best to keep her voice steady.

'I know your game. Well let me tell you, Rory Loates has bigger fish to fry than a nanny who plays bows and arrows.' Jackie slammed down the receiver.

Wincing, Stella shook her head and also hung up. A shadow moved in the courtyard. Sparky, who had been snoozing by the boiler, began to bark, then pattered outside to investigate.

'What's wrong? Sparky, heel,' Stella called out. The dog was now outside the cow byre, barking excitedly.

Fearing an intruder, Stella tiptoed

into the study. Her work was in disarray. Photos and notes were strewn across her desk.

'What's all the noise about?' Rory took a startled step backwards. 'I hope you don't intend using that on me.'

'Sorry.' Stella lowered the umbrella she had snatched out of the stand. 'I think a fox might have got in. I left the door open.'

'What a mess.'

'Nothing I can't deal with. There was a call for you,' she said.

'Jackie?'

'I'm afraid so.'

Sparky raced into the study and sniffed at Rory's work boots.

'We weren't expecting you back so soon.'

Rory flung his leather jacket over the back of a chair. 'No need to go into details, but my high-profile interview is off. What's for dinner? All I've had today is a cup of coffee and half a bun.'

'I have to see to Pamela first. She was having a rest.'

'I'll see what I can find in the kitchen.'

'Did I hear Rory's voice?' Pamela greeted Stella.

'Yes.'

'Who was the other man with him?'

'What other man?'

'I heard a man's voice. On the telephone?' Pamela looked uncertain.

'I didn't hear anything. Would you like some help getting up?' Stella asked, anxious to change the subject.

'You go on downstairs. I'll join you shortly.'

Rory had laid the table with a red-and-white-checked cloth and placed a vase of spring flowers in the centre. 'I'm reheating some chicken in wine sauce and I've taken out the ice cream. It'll be nice and gooey for later. How's my mother?'

'She'll be down in a minute.'

'There's a jug of juice, or some wine if your prefer.'

Stella chose orange juice and Rory poured out a glass of red wine, then checked on the simmering chicken.

'How's Fenella?' he asked.

'I've been busy organising our girls' day out. Fenella's already been on the telephone jogging my memory.'

'As a family we do seem to be taking advantage of you.'

'My grandfather and Amy have gone off to Spain, so for the moment the Loates are the only family I have in this country.'

'You lost your parents when you were eleven?' Rory enquired. 'If you don't want to talk about it I understand, only Fenella mentioned it to me when I was driving her and Tom back to school.'

'They were in South America. I don't really know what happened; I don't think anybody does. I went to live with my grandfather and his second wife. It was Amy who nurtured my interest in photography. I went through a wild phase in my early teens,' Stella admitted. 'That's why I understand how Fenella feels. I was missing my mother, and I think Fenella is too.'

'Should we tell June about this?'

Rory asked. 'I know I've asked you before, but if you think it's serious then perhaps she should come home.'

'Not yet. Fenella's a well-balanced young girl and I think she appreciates what her mother's doing.'

'Thank goodness Tom seems settled.'

'I'm not so good with young boys,' Stella said with a smile. 'If he throws a wobbly, then the ball's in your court.'

'Am I interrupting anything?' Pamela asked from the doorway.

Stella got to her feet with a guilty start. 'Nothing at all,' she insisted.

'Sit down, Mother, and I'll serve up.' Rory drew out a chair.

Their early dinner was a lively affair.

'Are you sure I can't tempt you to a glass of this full-bodied red?' Rory waved the bottle at Stella. 'You'll have to be quick. Mother's already into her second glass.'

'I only had a small top-up,' Pamela objected.

'I need a clear head for the morning,' Stella insisted.

Rory recorked the bottle. 'I suppose I should follow your example.'

'Who can that be at this time of the evening?' Pamela said as the telephone began to ring. 'I hope it's not that female who's been making a nuisance of herself.'

'If it is, I've a few sharp words to say to her.' Rory got to his feet.

'Poor Rory.' Pamela smiled gently. 'I can't imagine what any woman would see in him, can you? He works odd hours, he can be a bully, and he doesn't tolerate inefficiency.'

Rory rushed back into the kitchen. 'It's Tom,' he gasped. 'He's been in an accident.'

13

Blue lights arced the night sky.

'I'm sorry, madam,' a police officer said, stopping their car, 'the road is closed.'

'Officer,' said Rory, leaning forward from the passenger seat, 'my name is Rory Loates.'

The policeman's eyes widened. 'Sorry, sir, didn't recognise you there. As I was saying to the young lady, there's been an accident.'

'We received a telephone call saying my nephew Tom is involved.'

'In that case, sir, go right through.' The policeman removed the barrier.

'You'd better wait here, Stella,' Rory said as he got out of the car. 'I'll go and see what's happening.' He strode off into the darkness.

Stella accosted a passing ambulance man. 'Excuse me, what happened?'

'A driver did an emergency stop.

Think it was a rabbit.'

'Has anyone been injured?'

'The driver of the first car. Nasty case of whiplash. Sorry,' he apologised, 'we've got another call.'

Stella's dinner churned in her stomach. As she hadn't been drinking, she had volunteered to drive after Rory received the telephone call.

'Don't worry about me,' Pamela urged. 'Off you go.'

Rain began to fall and Stella wound up her window. Through the windscreen, blurred images passed to and fro. She glanced at her watch. She had been parked for over half an hour. Surely it couldn't take this long to find one small boy?

Stella opened her door and the next moment a small body hurled itself into her arms. She could feel the rapid beat of his heart against hers.

Rory came up behind him. 'No injuries. In fact,' he added, crouching down and patting Tom's back, 'our boy's a hero.'

'I didn't do anything,' Tom insisted.

'But I was scared.'

'You were very brave.'

'What happened?' Stella demanded.

'Let's get home first. Come on, hero. It's way past your bedtime.' With a brief, 'Tell you later,' Rory bundled Tom into the back seat.

'He's wearing cricket whites,' Stella said in a low voice.

'That's what he'd been doing, playing cricket. Hang on while I telephone my mother. I don't want her worrying.'

Stella turned down Knight's Walk and drove carefully along the bumpy road. Tom stirred and rubbing his eyes sat up.

'Nearly there,' Rory informed him as the welcoming lights of Minster House came into view. There was a bright beam of light as the kitchen door was opened and Sparky raced out.

'Everyone inside,' Rory ordered.

'Take Tom upstairs, Stella,' Pamela suggested. 'Rory, you'd better telephone the school and let them know what's going on. I'll put the kettle on.'

Leaving Tom to soak in the bath, Stella turned on his bedside light and found him a pair of clean pyjamas.

'The hot water bottle's ready,' Pamela called up the stairs.

Stella placed it in the middle of the bed, then going in search of a warm towel knocked on the bathroom door. Moments later a sleepy Tom was tucked up in bed. He hadn't objected to a hug and kiss from Stella, and soon she could hear him breathing deeply. Tiptoeing from the room, she picked up his discarded clothing and made her way back downstairs.

'I've telephoned the head teacher,' Rory explained. 'He's full of apologies. He wouldn't usually agree to Tom going out for the afternoon without telephoning us first, but he couldn't get through.'

'That was probably Jackie blocking the line,' Stella explained.

'It delayed Tom and he missed the school coach, so he got a lift to the match from one of the teachers.'

'But what happened?' Stella demanded.

'I was talking to the authorities; that's what took me so long.'

Restraining the impulse to shake further information out of Rory, Stella was about to repeat her question when Pamela stifled a yawn. 'You can tell me your story in the morning, Rory. All I need to know is that my grandson hasn't been injured. Good night, Stella. Thank you for coming to our aid. Yet again I don't know what we would have done without you.'

Stella sat down at the table. 'We forgot to put the ice cream away.' She looked at the congealed tub of raspberry ripple.

'I never did eat mine.' Rory picked up his discarded plate and scraped the contents into the bin. 'Fancy a biscuit?'

'I'd rather you told me about Tom.'

'Right. Yes. The cricket match was a friendly, and as far as I could make out there was some confusion over dates, so when the coach turned up to collect the team no one was ready.'

'But Tom wasn't involved in the accident?'

'No. The teacher driving him stopped to help. Wires then got crossed and we were told that Tom was involved in the accident. The paramedics said he was a great help telling them the names of the boys in the various vehicles. I gather more were following on behind the car that braked.'

Stella sipped her coffee. 'I'm glad I didn't join you in that glass of wine,' she said.

'When I think what could have happened, it brings me out in goose bumps.'

'Does Tom have to go back to school tomorrow?'

'I'll drive him over if they insist, but I think they'll be glad we're not going to make a fuss.'

'Does Fenella know?'

'I presume someone will tell her. I know it's not Jackie's fault, but the trouble that woman has caused is nobody's business. If she hadn't been blocking the line none of this confusion would have happened.'

'You can't blame her.'

'Next time she telephones you have my full permission to tell her to stop calling.'

'Was your relationship serious?'

'We went out together, but only casually.'

'I have a big day tomorrow and an early start, so if you'll excuse me I think I'll follow Pamela's example and turn in.'

'What sort of job is it tomorrow?'

'A model shoot.' Stella grimaced.

'More fragile egos?'

'No one ever keeps to schedule. Things overrun. The venues change. I've turned up expecting to take background pictures for a summer catalogue to find I'm knee-deep in ski wear.'

'Our chosen careers have a lot in common.'

'You've got more people jumping to your beck and call than I have,' Stella said with a wry smile. 'I'm the freelance and I do the jumping. I'll collect my notes from the studio so I won't disturb you later.'

Before she realised his intention, Rory put out a hand to detain her. His lips grazed her forehead. The gesture was no more than a friendly embrace, but it left Stella feeling as though the tips of her fingers were on fire.

'I've one or two things to catch up on too, and that was one of them.' His voice sounded as husky as hers had been earlier.

'You didn't have to kiss me,' Stella protested.

'It's something I've wanted to do for quite a while.'

'I don't like being taken advantage of,' Stella began to say.

'Have I taken advantage of you?'

She stiffened at the sound of the ringing telephone. 'You'd better answer it. It might be Jackie.'

★   ★   ★

There was no sign of Rory in the kitchen when Stella returned half an hour later, having collected her work

139

from the byre. The debris had been cleared away and the surfaces were spotless.

Hurrying upstairs to her room, she laid out her plans for the morning and worked on them until well into the small hours. After only a few hours' sleep, she stumbled downstairs to find Tom seated at the kitchen table demolishing toast and marmalade.

'Rory's been called away. He said to tell you he probably won't be back until the weekend. I can stay off school until then. Cool, isn't it?'

With a forehead that still tingled from his kiss the night before, Stella agreed it was, although her feelings about Rory Loates were far from cool.

14

The telephone rang several times during breakfast.

'Is Tom OK?' Fenella demanded.

'No problems,' Stella assured her. She replaced the receiver only to have the telephone immediately shrill into life again. Her photo shoot had been brought forward.

'Go,' Pamela urged. 'We'll manage.'

'What about your ankle?'

'Tom can run any errands. Take my car.'

The telephone rang again. 'Who?' Stella heard Pamela say as she went upstairs for her coat. 'Jackie? I'm sorry, my son isn't here.'

Blowing a kiss at Tom, who was sitting at the breakfast table studying his cricket statistics, Stella loaded up Pamela's car with her equipment and headed for the main road.

Haverton House stood on the county border and the postcode differed from that of its neighbours. As Stella slowed up at a roundabout, uncertain which exit to take, a white van overtook her, hooting furiously. Stella's glare turned to a smile as she recognised the driver as one of her favourite technicians. He pointed to the second exit left and Stella followed his vehicle down the narrow lane.

Huge cables stretched across the lawn and contractors' vehicles blocked the drive.

'Stella, darling,' the shoot manager, Barney, greeted her. 'Thank heavens you're here. I am on the verge of a nervous breakdown. You're starting off in the library. Get yourself a coffee and meet me there in fifteen minutes.' He inspected his watch. 'That's if I'm not in police custody by then for throttling Kaylee.'

'Up to her usual tricks, is she?' Stella raised her eyes at the mention of the name. The last Stella had heard, Kaylee was involved with her ex-fiancé Mark.

'By the way, we've clashed with some art evaluation people,' Barney explained. 'Not sure who's here on the wrong day, but as a compromise they've promised to stay out of our way and we've agreed not to encroach on their business. It should work if we stick to the timetable. Some hope. Anyway, do your best, darling. I know I'm asking the impossible.'

'You always do.'

'Now, now.' He wagged a finger at her. 'No, not there,' Barney bellowed, striding off in the direction of a cloth-capped deliveryman.

Stella made for the catering van, where she learned to her dismay that Mark Dashwood was expected on set. She finished her coffee before unloading her equipment and heading for the library.

The room smelt of musty books. Stella ran her fingers over their spines, enjoying the feel of the tooled leather. Her remit was to personalise the background shots. She began to check out the conditions in the library.

One or two the friendlier models smiled and exchanged a few words. As usual there was a lot of hanging around, and they seemed grateful to have a chance to alleviate the boredom.

'What's the hold-up?' Stella enquired, noting the movement of the sun through the large windows. Natural light could significantly alter her settings.

'Kaylee,' they said, grimacing.

As there was no sign of Barney, Stella ambled out and onto the lawn. 'I'll be taking exterior shots for my records,' she said, 'if anyone needs me.'

The mellow stone of the house basked in the warm sunlight. This was the sort of day Stella enjoyed. She snapped away. Lost in her work, she narrowly avoided tripping over a snaking cable and immediately fell into a pair of masculine arms.

'I heard you'd be here today.'

She blinked up into Mark's handsome face.

'How are you?' he asked when she made no attempt to return his greeting.

'If you'll excuse me, I have to get on.'

'Surely you can spare a few moments to talk to me?'

Knowing she was in danger of scowling, Stella did her best to smile at Mark. It would do her reputation no good if she gave in to her temptation to tell him exactly what she thought of his attempts to blacken her name.

'How's Kaylee?' she asked.

'I hope that's not jealousy I can hear in your voice,' Mark responded with a smug smile.

Stella began to wonder what she could ever have seen in so conceited an individual. He displayed no remorse for his callous treatment of her, but actually seemed to believe she was jealous of his new relationship.

'I've heard a rumour about you and Rory Loates,' Mark persisted.

'Then you've heard wrong.'

'He and Jackie James have got a thing going.' Mark's smile didn't reach his eyes. 'And I don't think you would come off best if there were a showdown.'

'I'm far too busy at the moment to give any thought to showdowns of any nature.'

'You needn't think it worries me.'

'What doesn't worry you?' Stella frowned.

'You and Rory.'

'Stella?' Barney had borrowed a megaphone in an attempt to attract her attention. 'I said the library not the west lawn. What do you think you're playing at?'

'I have to go.' Stella swept past Mark.

'Sorry,' Barney apologised, 'only I thought you needed rescuing.'

'I did, and thanks,' Stella replied.

'I know gloating isn't in your nature, but the delectable Kaylee is in a bad mood. You may like to stay out of her way.' Barney leaned in closer. 'She was watching the pair of you from an upstairs window and nearly fell out 'cause she was trying to hear what you were talking about.'

'Thanks for the warning.'

'If you want to do your stuff in the

library now, you shouldn't be disturbed. We'll be in the conservatory. We're doing our best to follow the set route in order not to clash with the art people, but all this avoiding each other is giving me a headache.'

'Will they be needing the library?'

Barney glanced at his clipboard. 'It's not on my list.'

The technicians were clearing out the last of their equipment as Stella approached the library.

'All yours. You don't want an assistant, do you?' one of them asked, wincing at the sound of raised voices from the direction of the conservatory.

''Fraid not.'

'Oh well, once more into the fray,' he said before reluctantly shuffling off towards the source of the disagreement.

Stella opened one of the windows to let in some fresh air. The library faced south and the room was growing warm.

The wooden floors creaked comfortingly as she moved around taking her shots. Dusting the surfaces, she moved a vase of spring flowers to a better angle and zooming in, highlighted them. It helped to have a working knowledge of the location to add to her portfolio and she spent several moments adjusting the images, which she would later download onto her computer.

She liked to work with all media when it came to taking pictures, but in her experience modern technology required less preparatory work and could be completed in half the time. Glancing at her watch, she was surprised to see it had taken over an hour and a half to get all the shots she wanted.

Stacking her heavier equipment by the door, she again strolled out into the gardens. The morning session had overrun, but she sensed it was coming to an end due to the increased activity around the catering van. The smell of frying sausages made her stomach rumble. Glancing up at the house, she caught a glimpse of a man leaning over a balustrade. As he straightened up, the sunlight caught the while petals of the rose in the buttonhole of his camel-hair coat. She raised her camera and snapped a quick shot. The man gave a startled look in her direction, then ducked down from view.

15

On the drive home Stella couldn't get Buttonhole Man out of her mind.

'Stella!' Tom was jumping up and down in the courtyard, having waited for her. 'Mum's home. Isn't it brilliant?'

Standing behind him was June, wearing a shimmering turquoise top, black leggings and a shocking pink sparkly scarf. Throwing open her arms, she kissed Stella on both cheeks.

'I'm so sorry my son has been such a nuisance. I do hope he apologised.'

'Stella was ace. Rory too.' Tom displayed no after-effects of the previous day's trauma, for which Stella was relieved. 'And what happened wasn't my fault.'

'That is not an apology,' June reminded him sternly.

'Sorry, Stella, if I caused you any trouble.' A look of dread crossed his face. 'You don't want a kiss from me too, do you?'

'I suppose that will have to do for an apology?' June queried with a look at Stella. 'If Stella is gracious enough to accept it.'

Stella took pity on Tom. 'I accept. And I only kiss boys on their birthdays.'

'I must remember to tell Rory,' June murmured with a wicked twinkle in her eyes. 'His birthday is in July. Now off you go, Tom. Girl talk.' Looking relieved, he snatched a banana out of the fruit bowl and scampered away. 'Ma is having a rest,' explained June.

'She did say she could cope with Tom for the day,' Stella was anxious to explain.

'It's not what you bargained for, is it, when you took the job of companion to my mother,' June sympathised. 'I've made tea and found the biscuits. I haven't been here long myself. When the head teacher telephoned to let me know what had happened, it was the middle of the night in Dubai. I caught the first flight home.' She poured out two mugs of tea. 'Now, tell me all that's been going on.'

'It's much as you see,' Stella replied, wondering where to start.

'You're sleeping in my old room?'

'Is that OK with you?'

'Of course it is, but why did you move out of the cow byre? Didn't you want your own space?'

'Rory moved back.'

'So my little brother's home, is he?'

'For the moment.'

A shadow crossed June's face. 'And Ma? I would have thought she would be up and about by now.'

'The doctor said her ankle is taking longer to heal than he would have liked,' Stella admitted.

'I'd better have a word with him. I'm so pleased you're here.'

'How long are you staying?' Stella asked.

'My return ticket is open-dated. I need to have some time with Fenella, and that's another problem.' June frowned. 'Tom tells me she's been mixing with a different set of girls at school. Do you know anything about it?'

Not wanting to betray the girl's confidences, Stella said, 'I think she misses you more than she's prepared to let on.'

'She is at a delicate age,' June agreed. After a short hesitation she said, 'The thing is, Andrew and I are getting back together.'

'That's wonderful news.'

'I haven't told the children yet.'

'I won't breathe a word,' Stella promised.

'Andrew's tour of duty doesn't end until late summer and I would like to stay out there with him until then. The children could come and visit in the holidays but there's not much for them to do. With so much going on in their lives, I thought staying with their grandmother would be less disruptive, but I didn't realise I'd miss them quite so much.'

'I've actually booked a day's beauty treatment at a health club this weekend for Fenella and myself. We were going to get our nails done and perhaps have a massage.'

'Would you mind terribly if I took your place?' June asked. 'I know it's an awful cheek, but I promise I'll treat you to a pamper day at my expense to make up for it.'

'There's no need to make up for anything,' Stella enthused. 'It was a treat I promised Fenella after we had a little chat. She said much as she loves Tom and Rory and her grandmother, she missed the feminine touch.'

'It's settled then.'

'Having you home has lifted a weight off my shoulders.' Stella smiled at June.

The telephone began to ring.

'Wretched thing. I'll take it. Finish your tea. Minster House; my name's June Waugh if you must know,' she spoke after a short pause. 'Who are you?'

Stella rose to her feet. 'Bath,' she

said, indicating her intention.

June put her hand over her receiver. 'Who is Jackie James?'

'Ex-girlfriend of Rory's. Good luck.'

Stella smiled as she heard June telling Jackie, 'Rory is my brother, and if he isn't returning your calls perhaps he doesn't want to speak to you.'

'Stella, is that you?' She heard Pamela calling out her name from the sitting room and pushed open the door.

'I thought you were upstairs,' Stella said.

'I prefer being downstairs during the day. I like to know what's going on. It's as well I was here. Tom had his headphones on and he didn't hear June banging on the door. Isn't it good news about her and Andrew?'

'I understand we've been sworn to silence.'

Pamela picked at a stray thread on her rug. 'The thing is, we're running out of bed space. I suggested June sleep in Fenella's room, but the silly child is annoyed with Tom for reading her diary, and she's only gone and locked the door and taken the key back to school with her.'

Pamela looked expectantly at Stella. 'You want me to move out?'

'Only into the extension. Would you mind?'

'What about Rory?'

'He won't be back before the weekend, and by then hopefully we'll have got the key off Fenella. It's such a nuisance. I'll never complain about feeling lonely again.'

'The extension is fine with me,' Stella said.

'I wouldn't want you to think I was banishing you now the family are back,' Pamela said quickly.

'The thought never crossed my mind.'

With Tom's help Stella stacked Rory's belongings into a corner of the living room. June remade the bed for her, all the while apologising for the disruption she had caused. 'I could have slept here,' she insisted.

'Your place is in the house with your son and your mother. Besides, didn't you say your husband was going to call tonight?'

'You're a star. If this health spa is any good, what say we treat ourselves to an exclusive day?' June suggested.

'I'd like that.'

'Good.' She kissed Stella on the cheek. 'I'll leave you to get on. If you get lonely, come on over. We're having a really exciting evening — shepherd's pie and Tom's new video game.'

With everyone out of the way, Stella worked on until late in the evening. Her prints had come out well and she was pleased with them. She caught her breath as she clicked on the last shot. It showed Buttonhole Man on the balustrade. The image was blurred, but Stella did the best she could with the focus control, then printed out a copy before saving the remainder to the agency files.

Tidying up her desk, she pulled out an envelope and slipped the photo into it. Another photo fell out of the folder.

It was the picture she had taken at Jenkins Gallery. There was no doubt about it: it was the same man in both photos.

Making a mental note to do more research in the morning, Stella switched out the light. Snuggling down, she fell asleep.

★   ★   ★

Stella was jerked awake by a loud thump, then another crash. Her hand hovered over the bedside light. If she turned it on the intruder would know she was awake. She knew exactly what he was looking for — the photograph.

Remembering the small torch that she kept in her handbag for emergencies after the incident with the lights in the main house, Stella pushed back the sheets, and feeling her way carefully in the darkness inched across the room. Her bag was on the hook on the back of the door. Gritting her teeth, she undid the zip as quietly as she could, then extracted the torch. Fumbling around, she came across an aerosol of hairspray. Clutching both items firmly in one hand, she eased open the door with the other.

'What the hell is my stuff doing there?' Stella heard Rory say too late to stop her from switching on her torch, squirting hair spray into his eyes and yelling like a banshee.

Rory fell backwards with Stella on top of him just as the room was flooded with light. June stood in the doorway, surveying the scene.

'Where did you come from?' Rory gasped.

'I'm home,' June answered. 'You can kiss me later. Right now I think you have more pressing priorities. Stella, what are you doing?'

'I thought Rory was a burglar.'

'What on earth is that?' Rory wrenched the aerosol can out of her hand.

'Hairspray.'

'What pretty pyjamas, Stella,' June

interrupted. 'But I think you'd better go and find a dressing gown.'

Aware that her body was still crushed against Rory's, Stella scrambled to her feet and fled the room.

'Trust you to ruin things, June,' she heard Rory grumble as he kissed his sister. 'I was beginning to enjoy myself.'

'That's what I was afraid of,' June replied. 'And what are you doing here?'

'I asked first,' Rory retaliated. 'But if it's complicated, it's going to have to wait until the morning. Is the sofa in the house free?'

A suitably robed Stella reappeared in the living room. 'You can have your bed back.'

'I think not,' June said firmly. 'Rory, sofa, now,' she ordered her brother. 'Stella, back to bed.'

'It's best to do as she says.' With a wink in Stella's direction, Rory picked up his bag. 'See you in the morning. Sleep tight. By the way . . . ' He paused in the doorway.

'What?' Stella demanded.

'They *are* nice pyjamas. I particularly like the teddy bears.'

Blushing to the roots of her hair, Stella realised she was wearing an old pair of pink pyjamas that Amy had given her one Christmas. They were emblazoned with hearts and flowers and teddy bears exchanging kisses under sprigs of mistletoe.

16

'I'll fetch Fenella from school,' June offered over Friday morning breakfast. 'We can chat about things in the car. I telephoned the health club and they are happy for me to take your place, so that's Saturday fixed. We'll probably stay overnight; make a weekend of it.'

'What about Tom?' Stella asked.

'He's got a sleepover.' June sipped her green tea. 'By the way,' she said, flapping her hands at Stella, 'Ma's planning a holiday. She's going to visit her sister in Edinburgh. Have you met Doreen?'

'No.'

A rueful smile crossed June's face. 'Then you're in for a treat.'

Stella remembered Rory mentioning his aunt as having been second choice for the job of companion to Pamela.

'What's she like?' Stella asked.

'She's younger than my mother,' June

added delicately, 'in every way.'

'Pamela mentioned that she never married.'

'No one was brave enough to take her on. She's strong-willed and doesn't take well to authority. I like Doreen, but she's emotionally high-maintenance, and that's something coming from me.'

'When is Pamela leaving?' Stella asked.

'Tomorrow. Rory's agreed to drive her to Gatwick. He's arranged wheelchair transport to the aircraft so Ma won't have to walk down endless corridors.'

'How long is she going for?'

'As long as the pair of them can stand each other's company.' June crossed her arms. 'So, I expect you'll be pleased to have some time on your own.'

'I'm catching up well,' Stella informed her.

'Sorry about all that business with Rory,' June apologised. 'The pair of you did look funny rolling around the floor.'

'I was not rolling around the floor,' Stella protested.

'You could have fooled me. I'm only

teasing.' June patted Stella's hand. 'Rory didn't see the note on the kitchen table telling him about the revised sleeping arrangements.' June paused. 'I know it's none of my business,' she began, 'but you're not in any trouble, are you?'

'What sort of trouble?'

'Rory mentioned text messages and a break-in.'

'It might have been a fox.'

'Goodness knows this family's got enough skeletons in its cupboard to stock a teaching hospital, so you needn't worry about a thing. Whatever you've done, we're on your side.'

Stella blinked, touched by June's concern. 'To my knowledge I haven't actually done anything.'

'In that case we've nothing to worry about, have we? Change of subject. I suppose there's no chance of you and Rory getting together, is there?'

'You mean professionally?'

'I mean romantically.'

'No.' Stella hoped she wasn't too red in the face.

'Pity. I'd like you for a sister-in-law, and I know Ma and the children would welcome you into the family.'

'Rory tried to have me evicted on my first day here,' Stella pointed out.

'My brother can be short-sighted at times. Take that Jackie female, for example. I had to be quite sharp with her the other night when she began whining on about him not returning her calls. Best get on I suppose. I'll be using Ma's car today, if that's all right with you.'

After her talk with June, Stella's assignment at the garden centre overran and she was invited to stay overnight.

'You can have our daughter's old room,' the manageress explained. 'You don't want to go driving all the way back tonight, do you?'

'I haven't much left to do,' Stella admitted.

'Best finish up first thing in the morning then.'

'No problem.'

June took Stella's call. 'I'll get Ma's

home help to look after Sparky if you'd pick her up on your way home. Fenella sends her love.'

Minster House was eerily quiet as Stella let herself in. Her hosts at the garden centre had insisted on treating her to a light lunch in the café, and after talking to some of the customers to get a feel of the place, time had run away with her.

'Fancy a walk to clear away the cobwebs?' she asked Sparky, who trotted into the kitchen behind her.

Mention of the magic word galvanised the spaniel into action and she began to run round in excited circles. Stella clipped on her lead and, locking the door behind her, slipped the key into her pocket. At the sound of an approaching vehicle Sparky dragged a protesting Stella towards the four-barred gate.

'Where are you off to?' Rory asked.

'I thought we'd get a breath of fresh air.'

'I'll join you.' He was dressed in

cargo pants and a checked shirt with a jumper tied around his shoulders. 'The flight was delayed,' he explained. 'Air traffic control. Shall we head for the heath?'

They circuited the cow byre, then climbed over a rickety fence.

'Can you hear it?' he asked.

'A bird?' Stella asked.

'That's not any old bird. It's a Dartford warbler. It's quite rare. I used to come on nature rambles with my father when I was a boy. I think that's how I got my love of the great outdoors.'

'Did June join you?'

'Not really her thing. She liked parties and fashion magazines. What got you into photography?' Rory asked.

'I went through a rebellious phase,' Stella admitted. 'After I borrowed some money from Amy's purse without her permission, she decided I needed an interest. I was hanging around with a bad crowd and I'm ashamed to think of the sleepless nights I must have caused her.'

'It's all part of growing up,' Rory said.

'Amy promised me a camera if I completed a photography course being held at the local activities centre. She drove me over every week and as there was no way of getting back until she came to fetch me, I had no choice but to attend the session. The tutor was brilliant and I began to look forward to the lessons. We had a competition at the end of term and I got a special mention. Without my knowledge the tutor sent my still life to the local newspaper and they printed it. As promised, Amy bought me a camera. After that I was hooked.' She gave an embarrassed smile as she came to the end of her story. 'I can see why you're such a good interviewer,' she said. 'You don't interrupt.'

'Most people like the sound of their own voice,' Rory replied. 'Sorry, that sounded rude. What I meant to say was, it's important not to interrupt. It stops the flow.'

'What about you?' she asked.

'My father was chairman of a large media company and he got me the necessary introductions. Compared to you I've had an easy path.'

'You've built up your reputation yourself.' Stella felt the gorse grass swish against her legs. 'I'm sure you wouldn't have lasted long if you hadn't worked hard.'

'Walking and talking must be good for us. I've learned more about you in the last five minutes than I have the whole time we've been together at Minster House.'

'I'm sorry I came at you with the hairspray. I had some mad idea it might stop you in your tracks.'

'It certainly stuck my eyelashes together. It's always the same when my sister gets involved in things.'

'It wasn't her fault.'

'I hope you didn't suffer any lasting side effects.'

'A bruised knee, nothing more,' Stella assured him.

'Fancy a climb up to the tower? It's worth the effort. You can see for miles when you get to the top. Sparky,' Rory called out, 'this way. It was built as a lookout in Elizabethan times,' he explained, 'intended to spot any stray Spaniards on the horizon.'

'Aren't we too far inland?'

'I expect by the time they realised their mistake the thing was built.'

'It is a lovely view.' Stella paused, halfway up the climb.

'I have heard Sir Lancelot and his merry men bed-and-breakfasted nearby.'

'Now you're teasing me. Besides, that was Robin Hood.'

'I like to see you smile. I'm doing my best to make amends for my appalling behaviour on the day we met. I can't believe I was so pig-headed, but I was worried about my mother, and when Tom mentioned the mobile messages I totally overreacted.'

'Don't forget Mark Dashwood,' Stella pointed out.

Rory paused for a breather. 'Now

we're friends, you don't feel like telling me about it?'

Stella swung round to face him. 'Mark?'

'I mean the reason behind the threatening messages.'

'You've not going to start on all that again, are you?'

'I want to help. My opinion is, whoever you've photographed wants the picture back. Do we agree so far?'

'There are actually two photos taken on two separate occasions.'

'You didn't mention a second one.'

She briefly updated Rory. Again he didn't interrupt her until she got to the end of her narrative.

'I'm not out to scare you, but it's as well to be prepared. If you really have got something these people are after, then they sound the type of characters who won't stop until they've found it.'

'What do you suggest I do?'

'For the moment nothing. I'll make some enquiries.' He glanced at his watch. 'It's getting late. We'd better start back.' Slipping his hand through hers, they began to descend the hill.

'There's a car in the drive,' Stella said, shading her eyes as they approached Minster House.

'What?' Rory looked up from clipping on Sparky's lead.

'Darling.' A female waved as they rounded the corner. 'Where have you been? Hurry up and change. We're late.'

'Jackie?' Rory frowned in puzzlement. 'What's going on?'

'It's the awards ceremony tonight. Surely you can't have forgotten? You're in line for the Globe.'

17

Stella greeted Amy's house agent with a smile. 'Mr Skinner. I hope you're well?'

'Very, thank you. I'm a new grand-father,' he announced proudly, 'and it's a boy.'

'Congratulations.'

'I was sorry to drag you all the way down here, Stella,' he began, an uncomfortable expression replacing the smile on his face. 'The problem is, the last tenants made rather a mess of the place. As you know, I am meticulous about the letting conditions. I always check references, but this one slipped through the net.'

They were standing outside Fisherman's Rest Cottage.

'I could have coped with the paint stains on the wallpaper and the broken crockery,' he continued, unlocking the door, 'but unfortunately the back door has been damaged and the bathroom fittings are in a state too. It was most remiss of me not to have carried out further checks, but my wife wasn't well and we had our granddaughters staying while my daughter was in hospital having the baby. Our established routine was shot to pieces with unfortunate results.'

'I'm sure it's nothing we can't fix.'

'With the summer season coming up and bookings beginning to take off, I wanted you to take a look at the cottage before we proceed.'

'How long would it take to put things right?' she asked.

'I could start getting quotes immediately.'

'Get onto them as soon as possible, Mr Skinner. If you have any problems refer them to me.'

Mr Skinner looked relieved. 'That is a weight off my mind. I really have been most worried.'

'Don't give it a second thought,' Stella stalled him, fearing he was about to launch into another round of beating himself up.

'Will you be staying over?' he asked.

'For a little while.'

'Then I'll make sure the locks are changed.'

Still offering profuse apologies, Mr Skinner backed out of the cottage, finally leaving Stella alone. She plumped up a few cushions and straightened the ornaments on the windowsill. To her surprise they hadn't been broken. Stella had driven straight down to Devon after receiving Mr Skinner's telephone call early that morning.

'How long will you be away?' June had asked. 'Only, I'm thinking of taking the children back to Dubai for a short holiday. Andrew has the option of extending his contract. Now would seem as good a time as any for the children to visit. They need to see their father, and as the Easter break is coming up I would only be taking them out of a school a few days early.'

'I should have checked on my

grandparents' property before now, but I've been so busy. I hope to be back within the week.'

'You take on too much,' replied June. 'You've got your job; you are companion to my mother; you've inherited two teenage children, a dog, and a difficult landlord in the shape of my brother; I'm always interfering; and on top of that you're looking after a cottage in Cornwall.'

'Devon, actually,' Stella corrected her.

'Same thing.' June shrugged.

'I shouldn't let the locals hear you say that,' Stella advised.

'Is Fisherman's Rest Cottage as romantic as it sounds?'

'It's where I grew up. The village is sleepy and unspoilt. It attracts a lot of writers and artists and people who like the peace and quiet.'

'I don't know if it would suit me,' June replied.

★   ★   ★

Stepping out into the cobblestone street, Stella decided to walk up to the market for provisions.

'Back again, young Stella?' Sid the baker greeted her. 'Everything half price this late in the day.'

'I'll have a cob loaf and the last of your scones.'

'A very good choice, madam. Can I interest you in some of my wife's raspberry jam to go with the scones?'

Stella got out her purse as she watched him load jam, cream and a pat of rich golden butter into another bag. With a wink he slipped two doughnuts into another bag. 'On the house,' he said, leaning forward confidentially.

'Sid?' a voice floated through from the back room. 'Who is that you're talking to?'

'The other lady in my life, my cherub,' he responded.

A rotund female shaped very much like a cob loaf bustled through, her frown turning to a smile as she recognised Stella. Enveloping her in a flowery hug, she frowned at her husband. 'Are you deserting me for another woman?'

'It's Stella,' he protested, 'and I've loved her since she was a skinny teenager.'

'With braces on my teeth.' Stella managed to struggle free from Doris's embrace.

'I'd come after you with a rolling pin, Sid Masters,' Doris threatened, 'if you were thinking of being unfaithful.'

'Stella, can you live with the disappointment?' Sid put a hand on his heart.

'I'll bear up.'

'When are you going to find a husband of your own, Stella?' Doris demanded. 'A beautiful girl like you should be fighting off scores of admirers.'

'I'm afraid I'm not,' Stella confessed.

'What are the young men of today playing at? It took Sid two days to propose.' Doris squeezed Stella's elbow. 'I'm glad you didn't get together with the one you brought down here last summer. He asked Damerel to go swimming with him. Our granddaughter is only seventeen and still at college, and he was supposed to be down here with you. Anyway, what's past is past. We won't mention it again. Come to supper tomorrow. I'll do one of my fish stews.'

Clutching her purchases, Stella staggered back down the hill to the cottage. She was breathing heavily as she pushed open the front door. 'Who's there?' she called out, hearing a cough.

'Only me, miss. I'm the locksmith,' a voice replied from the kitchen. 'Planning a party?' He eyed the food Stella put on the table.

'I overdid things at the bakery,' she confessed.

'If there was a scone going begging, I wouldn't say no.'

By the time he'd finished securing all the locks, the light was fading from the day. 'I love this time of year, don't you?' He perched on a stool and sipped his strong tea before taking a healthy bite out of a cream-and-jam-laden scone. 'The village hibernates during the winter, but come spring the days lengthen and the air smells warmer.'

'You're quite a poet,' Stella laughed.

'I read some of my work at the festival last summer. Were you here?'

Stella shook her head. She had never missed one before, but Mark had wanted somewhere with night life for their holiday and they'd spent two noisy, hot weeks on a Greek island, crowded with European tourists all fighting for the best sun beds.

'Best be off.' The locksmith stood up and rinsed his mug in the sink. After showing her how the new locks operated, he packed up his bag.

'Please, take these.' Stella wrapped up the last of the scones and gave them to him. 'You can toast them for breakfast.'

Luxuriating in the bath an hour or so later, Stella's thoughts drifted off in a contented haze. After Rory — who was looking incredibly handsome in his dinner jacket — had driven off with Jackie to his awards ceremony, she had spent the evening watching a film. When the news had followed she had picked up the remote control to turn off the television, just as the presenter had announced that Rory's team had won the Golden Globe. The camera had panned onto his table. Jackie flung her arms around his neck and the flash-bulbs exploded as she kissed him.

Stella had texted congratulations. Everybody would want a part of Rory now and he wouldn't have time to get back to her, but she was doing her best to be grown-up about his relationship with Jackie James. When Mr Skinner's call came through, Rory had still not returned to Minster House.

Padding into her bedroom and open-ing the skylight to let in the chill night air, Stella hunted out a hot water bottle. She'd made up the bed with fresh cotton sheets, but they were cold and needed airing. Humming to herself, she plugged in the kettle, and while it was boiling checked her calls. There was nothing from Rory.

Outside she heard a car drive over the cobblestones. It was a rare occurrence, especially this late at night. Most people parked at the top of the hill. It was difficult to turn round at the bottom, and as the road went nowhere it made sense not to bother to attempt it.

Stella peered out of a window. Two red tail-lights disappeared into the evening mist. Turning back to the kettle, she filled her hot water bottle. She froze on the second step of the stairs at the sound of footsteps approaching her front door.

18

A shadowy shape began to hammer on the knocker. Stella peered through the letterbox.

'Net curtains are beginning to twitch,' Rory hissed. 'Open the door.'

It took Stella several goes to struggle with the stiff locks. Rory sidled past her in a flash and kicked the door shut. He tweaked her hot water bottle out of her grasp.

'What have we here?'

'Never mind that. What are you doing here?'

'Would you be more comfortable if I made us a hot drink while you got dressed?' Rory suggested. 'You might catch cold in your teddy bear pyjamas.'

Stella shot off upstairs, furious with herself for not slamming the door in Rory's face.

He pushed a mug towards her.

'Herbal tea. I found some doughnuts as well. I know I'm horribly late. I'm sorry.'

'I don't remember inviting you down to stay,' Stella pointed out.

'I've booked a room at the golf club.'

'Rory . . . ' Stella tried to shake the buzzing noise out of her ears. ' . . . explain.'

'June's message said you'd gone off to Cornwall.'

'Devon,' Stella corrected automatically.

'Anyway, I dialled one-four-seven-one on the landline.'

'Why?'

'I don't know, really. Anyway, I rang the number of the last call received. Although I managed to convince your Mr Skinner that I was a nice guy, he wouldn't give me your address, but he did give me his work details. So here I am.'

'It's nearly midnight.'

'I know.'

'And this isn't Mr Skinner's office.'

'I know that too. I went there first but it was closed up, so I started to look for clues in the holiday lets in his window.

It's not easy when you've only got a flickering streetlight to help. Then the wretched thing went out. This is where it gets really good.'

'It's gripping stuff,' Stella agreed, wondering when Rory was going to get to the point.

'The only place I could find open was the golf club. I asked them if they knew of any properties to let. The receptionist mentioned Fisherman's Rest Cottage and said I was in luck as Miss Bates was staying over, so here I am.' Rory sat back in his chair as if waiting for another Golden Globe.

'That still doesn't explain what you're doing here.' Stella frowned.

'I thought you might need help.'

'With what?'

'The break-in. I had the idea that Buttonhole Man was up to his old tricks.'

'You thought he was responsible for the damage to Fisherman's Rest Cottage?'

'June's note wasn't exactly detailed

but she did mention some trouble down here.'

'Why didn't you ring my mobile number?'

'I forgot to charge mine up. As there was no one at home and Mrs Watts is looking after Sparky, I jumped in my car and came on down here.'

They stared at each other in silence for a few moments.

'I think it's your turn to say something,' Rory said eventually.

'I don't know where to start,' Stella admitted.

'It is a tricky one,' Rory agreed. 'Now that I'm here, you could show me the sights.'

'Where's Jackie?' Stella demanded.

'I wondered when we'd get around to her,' Rory sighed.

'You owe me an explanation.'

'I do,' Rory agreed. 'I hate awards ceremonies,' he confessed. 'When the invitation came through, in a moment of weakness I agreed to attend. Then I forgot all about it. I was as surprised as you were to see her at Minster House. She seemed to think I'd agreed to go along with her. If it hadn't meant letting down the rest of the team, I wouldn't have gone.'

'Congratulations, by the way,' Stella said, 'for winning the Globe.'

'It was a team effort. The front man always gets the glory; that's why I hate the ceremonies. They don't reflect what goes on behind the scenes.'

'All the same, it's a great honour.'

'They're going to showcase the Globe in the crew room. It's given everyone such a boost.'

'You haven't answered my question. Jackie?' Stella prompted.

'What about her?'

'Where is she?'

'I've no idea. What do we do now?'

'Have another cup of herbal tea?' Stella suggested, wishing Rory's eyes weren't such a deep shade of brown.

'I'll pass, but I'll have that doughnut if you don't want it.'

Companionable village noises, the

creaky inn sign swaying to and fro in the breeze, and the distant swish of the sea drifted through the open window. Rory munched on his doughnut, and Stella knew the warmth welling up inside her was not from the reheated tea. It was an emotion she had never felt when she had been with Mark. Would Mark have raced down to Devon to make sure she was safe? Would he have enjoyed an impromptu midnight feast in a cottage kitchen that smelt of gutted fish?

'We could have a crab-sandwich picnic tomorrow and follow the river path to the source of the spring,' Stella suggested.

Rory leaned forward and cupped her hand in his. 'Great idea.'

'We'd better get some sleep.' With steely determination, Stella removed her hand from Rory's.

He stood up. 'Tomorrow morning? Ten o'clock?'

★ ★ ★

Doris had been agog with curiosity when Stella had explained why she needed a picnic the next morning. 'You told me you haven't got a young man.'

'You realise you've broken my heart,' Sid called over from where he was busy filling the shelves with the day's bake.

Doris stood on tiptoe to peer over Stella's shoulder. 'Is that him?'

Rory stood outside, studying their route on an old map.

'He's not my young man,' she insisted. 'He's the son of the lady whose house I live in.'

'What's he doing down here then?' Doris demanded. 'Shouldn't he be at home looking after his mother?'

'She's staying with her sister.'

'I see.' The two words were loaded with innuendo. Doris finished the sandwiches. 'There you are.' She gave them a pat. 'You won't find any fresher this side of Dartmoor.'

'Thanks, Doris.'

'Off you go. Enjoy your day.' She shooed Stella out of the shop.

A bright April sun dazzled from a brilliant blue sky. They took the path out of the village to where the river meandered through a gentle wooded forest.

'This is where Amy and I usually give up,' Stella confessed as they emerged onto a barren stretch of scrub heath land, 'and wander down into the village for a cream tea.'

'Hardly the spirit of the great white hunter,' Rory teased.

'We could battle our way through the gorse bushes and eat our sandwiches in the ruins of the old castle,' Stella suggested.

Rory shaded his eyes and looked in the direction of her pointed finger to where a battered ruin stood etched against the backdrop of a blue sky.

'It was a stronghold built to withhold invasion so the story goes,' Stella explained, 'but the invasion never happened.'

'Who ruined it?' Rory asked.

'The ravages of time I suppose,' Stella replied. 'Shall we go?'

By the time they reached the summit she was seriously out of breath. Rory, looking remarkably fresh, leaned against a collapsed wall waiting for her to catch up. The mournful wail of a nesting curlew floated towards them.

After they'd eaten in companionable silence, Stella sipped her drink while Rory packed up the remains of their lunch. 'Did you mention something about a cream tea?' he asked.

'We've only just finished lunch,' Stella protested.

'By the time you've done the down-hill run you'll be more than ready for sustenance. Come on. Last one to arrive pays.'

They stood on the cottage doorstep while Stella fumbled for her new set of keys.

'I didn't want it to spoil our day,' Rory began, 'but I received a call from the studio this morning.'

Stella looked up, a flutter of disappointment in her chest.

'I've a breakfast meeting schedule

first thing tomorrow.'

'You're going back now?'

'I don't want to lose an important commission.'

'I see.'

'When will you be coming home?' Rory asked.

Was Minster House home? Stella didn't know. She didn't know what to think anymore. Rory had rushed down to Devon because he had thought she was in trouble. He had stayed on and they had spent the day in the open air eating crab sandwiches and cream teas. And now as abruptly as he had arrived, he was leaving.

'I have to stay on,' Stella replied.

'Don't leave it too long.' His lips grazed hers in a gentle kiss. 'I can smell sunshine on your hair,' he said with a smile.

They looked at each other for a long, silent moment. Then with a brief wave, he turned away from her. Stella watched him trudge up the hill towards the golf club.

19

Amy's voice was full of outrage down the telephone line. 'Was it too awful for you, darling?'

'Mr Skinner has sorted out most of the problems,' Stella reassured her. 'To change the subject, how's Jennifer?'

'Blooming. So is Jim. We haven't done so much socialising in years. We never seem to get to bed before two in the morning. We've been given a new lease of life.'

'I'm pleased to hear it.'

'I'm fitter than I've ever been. I swim most days, and I walk to the market, and I've lost weight,' Amy announced. 'Jim's out right now, otherwise I'd put him on the line to have a word with you.'

'I only wanted to update you on all that's been going on here.'

'Then I'd better leave you to get on. *Hasta la vista*,' Amy finished their call.

★   ★   ★

Mr Skinner had taken to calling in once a day, and one evening leant a hand grouting the shower room.

'My wife is on a girls' day out with our daughter and a friend,' he explained, 'and as our son-in-law is looking after the children, there's no need for me to rush home.'

They had spent a companionable evening together broken only by an unexpected telephone call from Rory. 'Who was that man who answered the phone?' he demanded.

'Mr Skinner.' Stella watched him rinse out their equipment in a bucket. 'We've been tiling the shower.'

'I was wondering when you were thinking of returning. Fenella and Tom are back because June and Andrew had to take off for an unscheduled trip to America. As Fenella and Tom don't have visas, they came home.'

Stella could hear the background thud of Tom's music system.

'You'd never believe I bought him headphones for his birthday, would you? Tom,' he bellowed, 'turn it down.' There was a muffled response and a slight lessening in the volume of music. 'Can you hear me now?' Rory asked. 'When are you coming back?'

'I'll try to be home tomorrow.'

As Stella hung up, she realised she too was now referring to Minster House as home.

* * *

'All done,' Mr Skinner announced as he finished drying the last brush. 'I hope your young man wasn't too annoyed when I answered the telephone. He sounded suspicious. It's been years since anyone's been jealous of me.'

Resisting the urge to correct Mr Skinner of the widely held local belief that Rory was her young man, Stella suggested they retire to the golf club for a late supper. Sid and Doris were in the restaurant with various members of their family, and they insisted Stella and Mr Skinner join their table. When Mrs Skinner arrived their party began to grow in numbers, and the band hired for the evening decided to play on as no one showed any inclination to leave early.

'I've actually seen Stella's young man,' Doris announced during a break in the dancing when Stella had been unable to stop Mr Skinner from recounting his story about the telephone call, suitably embellished for his own gratification.

'What's he like?' Mrs Skinner demanded.

'Mrs Johnson, Stella's neighbour, said he presents those in-depth documentaries on television. His name is Rory Loates.'

'He's recently won an award,' another voice put in.

By the end of the evening Stella's face ached from smiling and assuring everyone there was nothing between her and Rory, but she suspected that despite her best efforts no one believed her.

When the manager of the golf club finally decided he had to close up and everyone stumbled out into the night, a steady rain was falling. Stella shivered in her thin dress.

'Borrow my umbrella,' Mrs Skinner insisted.

Stella did her best to keep the umbrella from blowing inside out as she braced herself against the stinging rain and the slippery cobblestones. Wishing she had thought to bring her torch, she stifled a shriek as a hand stretched out of nowhere and touched hers.

'Didn't mean to scare you,' Mrs Johnson said, hovering at her elbow. 'You've had a visitor. He said he was an acquaintance of yours and asked me where you were.'

'What did you tell him?'

'Nothing. There was something about him that didn't strike me as quite right.'

'Did he give you his name?'

'No. One thing I can tell you, though — he had a buttonhole in his lapel with a white rose in it.'

Her heartbeat going at triple rate, Stella let herself into the cottage. She fastened the door bolts and on shaking legs mounted the stairs. It was gone two in the morning before she drifted off to sleep.

★ ★ ★

The sun was low on the horizon by the time Stella turned into Knight's Walk. The rooftop of Minster House came into view. It represented a sanctuary of safety. She tooted her horn to let everyone know she had arrived.

'What's all the noise about?'

Standing in the kitchen doorway was a woman wearing a kaftan and chunky jewellery, and sporting spiky ash-blonde hair. 'Who are you?' she demanded.

'Stella Bates,' she replied.

'So you're the hired help.' The woman eyed her up and down. 'You're not what I expected.'

'And may I know your name?' Stella enquired.

'Doreen Soames. Lady Loates is my sister. I suppose you'd better come in. Put the kettle on and make some tea, will you?'

Sparky crept out of the door and trotting over to Stella, began nuzzling her toes.

'Glad someone is pleased to see me. Where is everybody?' She patted the dog.

Doreen was back in the doorway. 'I haven't got all day.'

Stella straightened up. 'I am not the hired help. After my long journey I would like a cup of tea too, so if you would care to put the kettle on, I'll join you when I'm ready.'

The hazel eyes crashed into hers and Stella thought she caught a glimmer of respect from the older woman. 'Rory said I'd have trouble with you,' she acknowledged.

'First round to me I think,' Stella murmured to Sparky, who looked in danger of winking at her.

'Do I spy crab sandwiches?' Doreen

pounced on the crumpled bag and sniffed. 'We'll have some now while Pamela's resting. The kettle is over there. I'll get a plate.'

With a sigh of defeat, Stella picked up the jug kettle and began to fill it with water.

20

'I've scheduled a rota.' Doreen pointed to the cork notice board. 'It's time to implement some efficient housekeeping. You've been guilty of letting things slip.'

Stella coughed as a piece of crab sandwich lodged in her throat.

'I hope you're not going down with a cold.' Doreen frowned. 'I've enough to do looking after Pamela. I don't want another invalid on my hands as well as looking after two teenagers.'

Stella swallowed some tea before she asked, 'Where are Fenella and Tom?'

A slight look of unease crossed Doreen's face. 'Rory's driven them over to visit Andrew's parents. They are down from Norfolk and they've rented a mobile home for a few days.'

'It's the first I've heard of it,' Stella said.

'It was a last-minute thing.' Doreen looked as though she wanted Stella to change the subject. 'If you must know, when the children discovered you weren't here and that I was taking charge of things, they decided to take up their grandparents' invitation to visit.'

'I see.' Stella retrieved the garden flowers Sid had given her and put them in a jar of cold water, all the while aware of Doreen watching her like a hawk.

'At least we'll have time be able to get to know each other,' the older woman said. 'I'm sorry I couldn't come down earlier, but when I saw the state of my sister's ankle I was adamant. There was no way I was going to let her undertake the flight home without me, and it's as well I was on hand to deal with things. We arrived at the airport to find the wheelchair had not been ordered. I had to assert my authority to get any attention at the check-in desk. The girl there was bordering on curt when I suggested she might benefit from some of my lifestyle advice.'

Stella was reduced to biting the inside of her cheek in an effort not to laugh. She was beginning to suspect that Doreen's forceful personality had a habit of rubbing people up the wrong way.

'These are good,' Doreen admitted grudgingly, taking another crab sandwich. 'Rory tells me you're a photographer?'

'I freelance.'

'Do you use the extension as a studio?'

'I have been until now.' Stella paused. 'Were you thinking of moving in?'

Doreen shook her head. 'I'm sleeping in the house. I need to be near my sister.'

'Is there room?'

'I'll share Pamela's bedroom. When I learned what was going on here I decided it was time I took charge. Now, I've done you a list of your duties.'

'Which we can discuss another time,' Stella said firmly.

'I beg your pardon?' Doreen gaped.

'I think it best to inform you now before there are any more misunderstandings that I have no intention of taking any notice of your rota.'

'Now see here,' Doreen began. 'I can't do everything on my own.'

'My arrangement with the lady of the house was to act as her companion. I assumed a few extra duties when her circumstances changed. It was my pleasure to do so but it was not part of our agreement.'

'Which is exactly why I've come to stay,' Doreen said. 'To help.'

'For how long?' Stella demanded.

Doreen's mouth was now set in a firm line. 'I am staying for as long as my sister wants me. I am family, after all.'

'In that case it might be better if I made alternative living arrangements,' Stella replied.

'You can't move out.' Doreen looked shocked.

'Why not?' Stella asked. 'I'm not family.'

'If you're thinking of moving out I

will make sure Aunt Doreen is on the first flight back to Scotland.'

The two women turned in surprise.

'Rory,' Stella greeted him with relief.

He eyed the remains of their supper. 'Crab sandwiches? Have you scoffed them all, Doreen?'

Doreen looked down at the crumbs on her plate. 'It's been one of those days and I was hungry.'

Rory continued to glare at his aunt.

'Sorry,' she mumbled.

'I meant what I said. I don't care where everyone sleeps; Stella stays.'

'I've never known such a fuss about sleeping arrangements,' Doreen gave in with good grace. 'I think I'd better go and see how Pamela is. The journey tired her out. That local cab driver needs taking to task. His vehicle smelt most peculiar, and I'm sure he drove us the long way round just to bump up the fare.'

'Her heart's in the right place,' Rory explained as Doreen grumbled her way upstairs. 'But don't let her walk all over you. I gather she's written out a duty roster.'

Stella nodded towards the sheet of paper pinned on the cork board.

A rueful smile softened Rory's lips. 'Tom and Fenella took one look and decided to visit their grandparents. I'm sorry I wasn't here when you got back, but I would have had a riot on my hands if I hadn't driven them over to see Andrew's parents.'

'What are we going to do?' Stella demanded.

'Carry on as before. Having Doreen here does make sense, and once we've settled down I'm sure everything will work out. My mother cannot cope with the demands of two active teenagers, and it's not fair to impose on you. Can I kiss you?' Rory asked.

Stella jerked back in surprise.

'Don't look so shocked. I'm relieved you're back. I wasn't relishing the prospect of being alone with Aunt Doreen. I think I'm in danger of falling in love with you.'

'No, you're not,' Stella insisted, 'and I'm not ready to fall in love with you or anyone else.'

Overhead they heard the thud of Doreen's feet as she began to unpack. A silky paw was placed on Stella's knee and two soulful brown eyes were raised to meet hers.

'Fair enough. But you're not moving out, are you?'

Stella stroked Sparky's soft head. 'I've no plans to.'

'Good.' Rory began to poke around the discarded paper bags. 'Do I spy scones, or has Doreen polished them off too?'

★ ★ ★

Over the next few days Stella saw little of Doreen. Her presence did lighten Stella's load, and she was able to get on with her photography work in peace.

Tom and Fenella's head teacher contacted her one afternoon to ask if she would consider doing the summer presentation photos.

'For our ceremony when the certificates of merit are awarded,' he explained. 'We like to acknowledge our students' hard work. Our regular photographer retired and Fenella suggested you.'

Touched by Fenella's confidence in her skills, Stella accepted the commission.

'By the way, Fenella's been displaying a lively interest in horticulture. We did a trip to a garden centre and she was asking really intelligent questions.'

The head teacher rang off as a taxi drew up outside. Standing on the doorstep, Stella was almost flattened as a gangly torpedo emerged from the back seat and hugged her. Then, as if remembering boys didn't do that sort of thing, Tom wriggled away. He greeted her with a casual, 'Hello.'

Fenella hovered behind him. Stella, past caring whether it was cool or not, hugged her too. 'My, look at you,' she said, admiring the sleek new hairdo.

Fenella went pink with pleasure.

'You'd better go and say hello to your great aunt.' Stella nudged them towards Doreen, who was standing behind her.

'Things will be back to normal now, won't they?' Tom asked earnestly.

'I'll do my best,' Stella promised. Her reply was greeted with two beaming smiles.

The children were full of plans for the weekend.

'There's an old car rally at the disused aerodrome on Bank Holiday Monday,' Tom explained. 'Rory is going to enter for the cup for the best renovation. I'm going to help him work on it.'

'More mess,' Doreen tutted.

'They have a barbecue in the evening,' Fenella put in, 'and a disco.'

'You're too young for such things,' Doreen replied.

'You'll stay on with Rory, won't you, Stella?' Fenella wheedled. 'I mean, you'll want to celebrate winning the cup.'

'We don't know that Rory will win,' Stella pointed out.

'Course he will,' Tom said with all the assurance of youth. 'There won't be another car there to touch his. I'm off to polish the paintwork.'

During the day, Pamela had taken to sitting on the patio on the far side of the house, and Stella hadn't seen quite so much of her since Doreen had taken over the household duties. Alone in the kitchen, Stella poured herself another cup of tea. Sparky began barking loudly in the courtyard.

'Quiet,' Stella called out through the window. 'You'll disturb Pamela.'

The dog ignored her. Stella strode into the courtyard as the dog began to growl at the garage doors.

'What is it? What's wrong?'

Stella looked round, fearing an intruder, but the courtyard was empty. She wrinkled her nose and coughed as a smell of burning caught the back of her throat. Sparky began scratching at the woodwork. Smoke was seeping out of the door cracks.

The garage was on fire.

21

'Rory!' Stella rattled the padlock. 'Tom! Somebody answer me. No!' she screamed as Sparky's tail disappeared through a gap in the wood.

She flung her body against frontage. The impact wrenched the padlock off its hasp. Stella hauled open the door. Smoke billowed out. Her throat felt as though it were on fire. Drenching her scarf in the water butt, she wound it over her mouth and nose and stumbled towards the body slumped by the side of the car.

'Come on, Rory.' She battered his leg with her bare knuckles, then rolled him over into a puddle of oily water. Sparky leapt into the driving seat of the car and began sniffing around the footwell.

'Sparky, get out of there!' Stella yelled.

Sparky barked and disappeared under the seat. Stella grabbed a bucket of water and hurled the contents into Rory's face.

'What the hell,' he spluttered.

Ignoring him, Stella dived into the car and grabbed Sparky's furry body. She stumbled outside, followed by a staggering Rory.

'Tom?' It scorched Stella's lungs to speak.

'Soldering. Spark fell on some plastic. Think I banged my head. Knocked myself out.' Rory doubled over.

'Where's Tom?' Stella shook his shoulders.

'Bedroom.' Rory surrendered to another paroxysm of coughing.

Stella shut a furiously barking Sparky in the cold room, then dialled the emergency services.

★ ★ ★

'To think I missed it all!' Tom was indignant with rage as the last fire engine departed. 'If you hadn't been drying your hair,' he said, turning on

Fenella, 'I would have heard Stella shouting for help.'

'You wouldn't have heard a thing; you had your earphones on,' she retaliated.

'Only because you don't like my music.'

'When you two have finished squabbling, there are dirty mugs to be collected and washed up,' Doreen ordered them.

'You know that bandage makes you look quite rakish, Rory.' Fenella leaned across the kitchen table and sniffed. 'Even if you do smell of scorched tyres.'

'You're not so fragrant yourself,' Tom chipped in.

After Stella had raised the alarm, everyone had rushed to her rescue. When the fire engines raced into the courtyard it was a smouldering mass of smoke and discarded water buckets.

'Thank goodness the fire didn't reach the house. Stella, how are you feeling?' Doreen asked, an unaccustomed softness to her voice.

'Shaky,' she admitted, trying to keep her hands steady. She was beginning to realise how close to disaster they had been.

'If it hadn't been for Stella we could all have been burned alive,' Tom put in with ghoulish glee. 'Sparky, too,' he added for good measure. He scooped up the dog. 'Say thank you to your saviour.' He waggled one of Sparky's paws at Stella. The dog leaned forward. Her wet whiskers tickled Stella's face as she licked her cheek. 'Now it's your turn, Rory.'

'I have no intention of licking Stella's cheek,' he said firmly in an effort to quell Tom's exuberance. 'She knows how grateful we are.' He directed a tired smile at Stella.

'All I can say is it's a good thing Pamela took a painkiller before I went out to bridge,' Doreen put in. 'She's sleeping like a baby.'

'Stella.' It was Fenella who now squeezed her hand. 'You've singed your hair. I'll wash it for you if you like,' she offered. 'I've got some lovely organic shampoo Mum treated me to on our health weekend.'

'Think we're out of the running for the cup,' Rory said to no one in particular.

'The car didn't catch fire,' Tom insisted.

'You can talk about it in the morning,' Doreen said. 'Stella needs her bed and so do you.'

'It's only half past nine,' Fenella protested.

Doreen checked the clock. 'Goodness, I thought it was much later than that.'

'I'm going to tweet my friends,' Fenella announced.

'Not before you and Tom have collected the mugs,' Doreen insisted. 'Stella, if you're not ready for bed, why don't you and Rory go into the sitting room? I'm sure you've lots to talk about, and I've laid out some dustsheets so you won't dirty things. Those firemen weren't too fussy where they put their boots. I had to have words with the one in charge about the mess.'

'Bet you did, Aunt Doreen,' Tom giggled.

'Get on with the washing up,' she retorted with the suggestion of a twinkle in her eye. 'You too, Fenella.'

'What are you going to do?' Fenella protested.

'I am going to make Stella and Rory a plate of sandwiches and a pot of hot, sweet tea. It's the best thing for shock.'

★   ★   ★

'Is that truly what happened?' Stella asked Rory when the two of them were alone in Pamela's sitting room. 'Solder really did fall on some plastic?'

'Why should I pretend otherwise?' The brown eyes were fixed suspiciously on hers.

Stella shook her head. How could she explain what she felt when she saw an ashen-faced Rory collapsed by the car? Her heartbeat still hadn't returned to normal.

'I don't know,' she admitted, her head in a whirl. 'So many odd things have been happening recently.'

'This wasn't odd,' Rory insisted. 'What happened was due to my carelessness. When I think of the damage I could have caused . . . ' His voice nearly failed as he added, 'I'm forever in your debt.'

'Anyone would have done the same,' she mumbled.

'No one else was around to do anything,' he pointed out. 'As usual, the family failed spectacularly in that department.'

'That's not fair,' Stella objected.

'I know it isn't,' Rory conceded. 'I am wholly to blame.' He looked down at his stained hands. 'I wonder if all this oil will ever come off.'

It still hurt Stella to breathe. The paramedics had wanted to take her to hospital for a check-up, but she and Rory had both refused.

'Nothing ointment and a hot bath won't cure,' he had insisted. 'Stella?'

Seated inside the ambulance encased in a thermal wrap, Stella had nodded her agreement.

'If you have any dizzy spells or any other symptoms, then you are to report to out patients immediately,' the chief medical officer advised her.

Stella promised she would before scrambling out of the ambulance and going to stand next to Rory. They held hands as they looked at the burnt-out doors of the garage, swinging sadly on their hinges and fanning the wisps of smoke still lingering in the air.

'Sustenance.' Doreen appeared in the doorway of the sitting room carrying a tray of sandwiches. 'I've sent Tom and Fenella upstairs. They're busy texting their friends, so I daresay it will be all over the county by tomorrow.'

'Stand by for a deluge of visitors,' Rory sighed.

Doreen sat down in an armchair. 'Funny how things go flat after a drama, isn't it?' She poured out some tea, then passed round the plate of sandwiches.

'Will the car be a write-off?' Stella looked at one of Doreen's sandwiches but left it on the plate. The thought of eating anything churned her stomach.

'I may be able to get it ready for the cup,' Rory replied. 'I'll check the damage in the morning.'

'That bump on the head's affected your judgement,' Doreen protested.

'You should see the state of some of the cars after they've been in a race,' Rory replied.

'I'm going to insist Tom doesn't help you again.' Doreen snapped a stick of celery. 'I wouldn't have a moment's peace if I thought you could all go up in flames.'

'Hopefully he'll be too busy telling his friends about the fire to bother polishing up paintwork.'

'If we do go to the rally,' Stella suggested, 'could we let Fenella stay on for the disco in the evening?'

Doreen threw her a scathing look. 'I don't know what's got into the pair of you. Half the house nearly burns down and you're discussing discos and car cups.'

'Fenella didn't lose her head when I roused her and Tom,' Stella said. 'They helped look after Sparky and make cups of tea. It would be nice to let her know we appreciate all she did.'

'I can't tell you how I felt when I saw all those blue lights flashing and an army of fire fighters stomping round the courtyard.' Doreen clutched at her chest.

'A disco isn't really my scene.' Rory pulled a face.

'Someone's got to act as chaperone,' Doreen insisted.

'Is there a hospitality tent for the adults?' Stella asked.

'It would mean staying on until the bitter end.' Rory cast a hopeful look at Doreen.

'Count me out,' Doreen said firmly. 'The days when I could dance until dawn are long over.'

'Let's sleep on it.' Rory stretched his legs.

Doreen began collecting up plates. 'If you've finished playing with that sandwich, Stella, I'm going to draw you a hot bath. Don't be long.'

'You were thinking the fire was the work of your Buttonhole Man, weren't you?' Rory said in a low voice after Doreen left the room.

'I'm not sure what I thought,' Stella admitted.

'Have you had any more contact with him?'

'No.' Stella turned away from the probing look in his eyes.

'I don't believe you.'

Her head shot up. 'Don't you understand the word 'no'?'

'I understand when you're hiding something.'

'I'm not hiding anything,' Stella insisted.

'Have it your own way. Go and have your bath before Doreen comes looking for you.'

Out in the hall the telephone began to ring.

'I'll answer it,' Rory said.

As Stella mounted the stairs she heard him say, 'June? That's right, no damage done apart from two burnt-out garage doors. The children were in their rooms most of the time. Mother was asleep and Doreen was out at bridge.' He paused. 'Stella's fine,' he assured his sister. 'She and Sparky saved the day.'

Stella padded down the corridor towards the bathroom. Doreen had laid out an enormous fluffy white bath towel, and Fenella had left some peach bath oil on the stool with a painted smiley note telling Stella to be as liberal as she liked. She poured a few drops into the bath; then, stripping off her smoky clothes, sank into the steamy water.

22

'We won!' Tom danced around the parade ground, waving the winner's rosette in the air.

'How did you manage to get it ready in time?' Stella asked Rory after the presentation.

'There wasn't much damage to the car itself, and after some minor cosmetic surgery and a late-night session she was as good as new.'

Stella looked towards the swarm of visitors gathered around the bright red paintwork, admiring Rory's workmanship.

'I helped,' Tom explained to a boiler-suited man. 'And we had a fire,' he announced importantly.

'Shall we leave him to it?' Rory said, looking at Stella. 'I'm parched.'

Stella looked over her shoulder. 'Where's Fenella?'

'The last time I saw her she was in the fresh produce tent. Doreen said she would keep an eye on her.'

'Did you know Fenella recommended me to do the photos for the school summer presentation?'

They sat down at one of the wooden tea tables in the marquee.

'Does that mean you won't be deserting us?' Rory asked.

'Why should I?' Stella replied.

'Putting out garage fires wasn't exactly part of your remit, was it?' The teasing light in his eyes softened his thoughtful expression.

'I feel a fraud,' Stella admitted.

'Now why are you beating yourself up?'

'I haven't seen much of Pamela recently, and I was originally supposed to be her companion.'

'Doreen has taken over that role. My advice is to let her get on with it. Now we need to talk.'

Stella's pulse quickened. 'What about?'

'Art scams. We've let things drift.'

Rory stirred his tea. 'I mentioned I had to pull out of an earlier investigation because my identity was in danger of being compromised, didn't I?' Stella nodded. 'It was disappointing, but you have to learn to accept these things. Anyway, a new director has taken up the project and he wants me on the investigation.'

'Isn't that rather dangerous?' Stella asked.

'I don't think so. I still have all my research notes, and most of the team I was working with have signified their willingness to be involved. It wasn't easy tracking down the crew, but from next week we should be up and running.'

'I see.'

'I mentioned your photos to the director and he would like to see them.'

'Aren't you placing everyone in danger by reviving the project?' Stella demanded.

'Why?'

Rory was being infuriating, playing

by his own set of rules, changing them when they suited his purpose.

'They hacked into my mobile. They know where I live, and it was you who wanted me out of Minster House because my presence was a threat to your family.'

Rory's brown eyes were fixed on Stella in an unblinking stare. 'There's something else, isn't there?'

'I think someone traced me down to Devon,' Stella was forced to admit.

Rory knocked the table with his knee, spilling tea everywhere. 'Why didn't you tell me?'

'Calm down. People are looking at us,' Stella hissed, attempting to mop up the liquid.

'I don't care if they are. I want the truth.'

'You remember Mrs Johnson?' Stella began. 'My nosey neighbour over the way? She said I had a visitor on my last night when I was out at the golf club. She mentioned he had a buttonhole with a white rose in his coat lapel, and the reason I didn't say anything was because I was rather preoccupied with your aunt descending on us and your garage catching fire.'

'The sooner I get hold of these pictures of yours, the better.' Rory glanced at his watch. 'It's a pity we can't leave now.'

Music started up in the background and people began drifting towards the disco tent. Doreen struggled through the tent flap, clutching armfuls of flowers.

'These were left over from the display,' she explained. 'Fenella won a junior prize for her miniature rock garden. I had no idea she was so talented. I'm off home now. I'll take Tom with me. He and some friends are coming back for a late tea. Will you look after Fenella?'

'Where is she?'

'She's gone to listen to the music. One of her companions is seriously weird, wearing rings in some very strange places.' Doreen hefted up a bunch of daffodils. 'Thought these would create a nice splash of colour for Pamela's sitting room. Yes, yes,' she said, glancing over her shoulder at the sound of raised voices behind her, 'I'm coming. I never knew young boys had such healthy appetites. You'll keep an eye on the girls for me?'

'It's not common knowledge, but the French police have expressed an interest in our investigation,' Rory said after Doreen had departed. 'They want to know if there's any connection with a similar fraud they've uncovered. They've had several instances of paintings being removed from properties, then later copies being passed off as originals.'

'Mr Jenkins's art gallery is hardly the Louvre,' Stella pointed out, 'and Haverton House is nothing special. Wouldn't a global scam be out of their league?'

'You'd be surprised. I've discovered the same people keep turning up at exhibitions and museums. It would be easy to set up an international network.'

Stella shivered. 'It all sounds rather menacing.'

'For the moment we're supposed to

be enjoying ourselves,' Rory insisted. 'How do you feel about helping me load my car onto a trailer?'

'That sounds like fun,' Stella responded with a wry smile. 'I thought you were driving it home?'

'The lights are unreliable and I don't want them going out on me, so I've arranged for the car to be delivered to Minster House.'

The disco tent was a crowded mass of loud music, strobe lights and gyrating bodies.

'We'll never find Fenella in all this,' Stella said, craning her neck. They battled their way through the throngs of youngsters, avoiding flailing arms and overactive legwork. Stella pointed to a girl wearing a striped miniskirt and pink tank top. 'There she is.'

'Fenella was wearing jeans when we left home.'

Stella threw Rory a pitying look.

'What have I said?' he asked.

'You didn't think any self-respecting teenager is going to attend a disco in her gardening kit, did you?'

'Has her hair always been like that?'

Stella waved enthusiastically in Fenella's direction.

'I told you it wasn't her. She's turned her back on you.'

'Don't you know it's terminally uncool to be seen waving to an old person?'

'Old?' Rory looked outraged.

'Anyone over twenty in this tent is ancient,' Stella assured him.

Rory watched the disc jockey start a new number. 'How much longer do we have to sit through this?'

'As long as it takes,' Stella replied.

It wasn't until two hours later when the music finally stopped that they were able to escape into the clear night air.

'That was way beyond brilliant,' Fenella enthused.

'Why does the music have to be so loud?' Rory grumbled.

'Because it does.' Fenella linked arms with Stella.

'Doreen told us about your rock

garden getting a prize,' Stella said. 'Well done.'

'I pressed some of those flowers you brought back from Devon,' Fenella explained with an embarrassed smile. 'They made a lovely display.'

A group of girls sauntering by sniggered. 'They made a lovely display,' one of them mimicked. Fenella flushed and unlocked arms with Stella.

'Friends of yours?' Stella asked.

'I know them,' she replied, exchanging a petulant look for her earlier smile. 'Why did we have to leave so early? I was having fun.'

'Ready?' Rory asked, returning from having checked that his car had been correctly dispatched on the trailer.

'S'pose so,' Fenella mumbled.

Stella shook her head at Rory as he looked about to ask a question.

The journey back to Minster House was completed in semi-silence, with Fenella sprawled out on the back seat checking her phone for messages.

'Thank goodness you're back,'

Doreen greeted them. 'It's been chaos here with parents collecting offspring, non-stop baked beans on tap, cars being delivered on trailers. Did you have a good time?'

Fenella slouched off towards the stairs. Doreen raised an eyebrow at Stella.

'I think it's a case of hormones,' Stella said, remembering her own teenage angst.

'Do you think I should have a word with her?' Doreen asked.

'Best leave her be,' Stella replied.

'I've got an early start tomorrow so I'll garage the car now.' Rory paused by the door and looked at Stella. 'I'd like to take those photos with me if you have them handy.'

Upstairs on the landing Stella heard Fenella's muffled voice through her half-closed bedroom door. 'Gardening is for grandmas,' she said with a mirthless laugh. 'Seriously gross.'

Hoping the girl wasn't being bullied into giving up something she was interested in, Stella made her way to her own room and unzipped her laptop case. She extracted the envelope from the back pocket; then, checking that the two photos were still there, she hurried downstairs.

'What photos are these?' Doreen asked, picking up the envelope Stella had placed on the table. 'Good heavens,' she laughed as they spilled out onto the table, 'that's Henry Lowring. I'd recognise that buttonhole anywhere.' She leaned forward to get a better look. 'And he's up to his old tricks, I see.'

23

The train pulled into the Gare du Nord. Amid much excited chatter, the group made its way along the platform, then out to the waiting coach.

'The city of light,' said one of the models. She inhaled, taking in the cafés and budget hotels. 'That smell always gets to me — garlic and Gauloise.'

Frantic hooting and the ferocious squeal of brakes drowned her words.

'For goodness sake, Caroline,' Barney said, yanking her back, 'they drive on the right in Paris.'

'Where are we staying, Barney? The Ritz?' she teased.

'Who cares as long as it's near the boutiques?' another model joked.

Barney did his best to usher the girls onto the coach. Stella's smile faded as someone sidled in next to her.

'Mark? What are you doing here?'

'I'm here with Kaylee.'

'I didn't see you on the train.'

'We travelled first class.'

'Where is she now?'

'She managed to talk Barney into providing a private car.'

Barney clapped his hands for attention. 'Is everybody here? Right, driver, then we'll be off.'

'April in Paris,' Mark sighed. 'The place for lovers, so they say.'

'Why aren't you travelling in the car with Kaylee?' Stella demanded.

'She brought so much luggage, there wasn't room for me.'

Stella looked determinedly out of the window. The Seine sparkled in the sunlight, with the imposing Eiffel Tower silhouetted against the skyline.

'What are you doing on this trip?' Mark asked.

'Barney wanted the Haverton House team on this shoot. I didn't think you were part of the team,' Stella replied.

Mark gave a shamefaced smile. 'I'm a passenger on this one — Kaylee's treat

— so I'll be able to spend my time in pavement cafés soaking up the atmosphere and watching the world go by. Care to join me?'

'I shall be working,' Stella pointed out.

'Not all the time, surely.'

The coach turned down a side street and came to a halt outside a small town house.

'I'll be handing out itineraries before dinner,' Barney announced. 'We are only here for two days, so any celebrating will have to wait until our last evening.'

'Fancy a drink later?' Mark asked. 'I'm sure Kaylee won't mind.'

'And I'm sure she will,' Stella replied firmly.

'Have it your own way.' Mark turned his attention to one of the models.

When Barney had telephoned the morning after the car rally to enquire if Stella were free to travel to Paris, she had leapt at the chance. Rory had left for London, and with Fenella still in a strange mood over breakfast Stella decided they needed some space, especially after Doreen's revelations of the night before.

'Henry was the one mothers advised their daughters to have nothing to do with. I suppose it's because he's half-French.'

'How do you know him?' Stella asked.

'We met at art school. I soon grew out of him. He was too flamboyant for my tastes. Had a ghastly mother — very well bred; thought she was a cut above the rest of us. Henry started wearing that rose in his buttonhole because he thought it gave him an air of charm.' Doreen made a noise at the back of her throat. 'He had charm all right, by the bucket load.'

Rory pocketed Stella's photos and advised Doreen not to repeat her story to anyone else.

'I don't gossip,' she replied, 'but I'll give you a word of warning: where Henry's involved there's usually trouble, so tread carefully.'

The fashion promotion was being shot at a château on the outskirts of

Paris, and next morning after breakfast the group headed out for the day.

On the bus Caroline smothered a yawn. 'I'm never at my best with early starts. Wake me when we get to our destination.'

The château was surrounded by a dried-up moat that was now a barren defence circling the walls. As their coach rattled over the drawbridge and under the portcullis, Stella felt herself being drawn back in time to the age of elegance and style.

The château was privately owned. The family chose to live in one of the estate properties, giving Barney and his crew freedom of the house and grounds. Everyone gathered round the catering van, discussing plans for the end-of-shoot party the next night. Montmartre seemed to be the favourite choice.

'I know this fantastic place,' Caroline enthused. 'If we book ahead we might be able to take it over for the evening.' She scurried away to find her mobile phone.

Barney shooed them along. 'Come

on everyone, back to work. I want to make the most of the light.'

Caroline came back. 'All booked. Hope Kaylee doesn't come,' she murmured in Stella's ear. 'Mark invited me to sneak off and join him for a drink last night. I'm not a keen fan of Kaylee's, but she doesn't deserve that. I don't think Mark's capable of being faithful to one woman.' She raised a horrified hand to her mouth. 'Sorry, I was forgetting about you and him.'

'It's history,' Stella replied.

Despite Barney's efforts, the second day's shoot overran.

'This is all Kaylee's fault,' Caroline grumbled. 'She wasn't in the best of humours, was she? Still,' she added, perking up, 'one of the benefits of being in this business is our ability to do a quick change. *Cinq* minutes, monsieur.' She beamed at the coach driver.

'*N'importe*,' he replied with Gallic gallantry.

'Hope that means it doesn't matter.' Caroline blew him a kiss.

'I think you'll find most red-blooded Frenchmen will let statuesque blondes get away with more than five minutes,' Stella said, nudging Caroline forward. 'But we'd best not put his patience to the test. I'd hate to have to walk to Montmartre.'

With a look of horrified agreement, Caroline rushed into their hotel.

After the coach dropped them off they caught the funiculaire up to the Sacré-Coeur, enjoying the panoramic views of Paris as the cab rose to the top of the hill.

'Follow me.' Caroline led them into the heart of Montmartre, then down a warren of back streets away from the bustle of the Place du Tertre to a crooked building decorated with painted murals.

Barney peered through a dusty window. 'Are you sure this is the right place? It looks very dark inside.'

As he spoke, a rotund red-faced man wearing a striped apron flung the door open and raised his arms in a gesture of welcome.

'Hello, Pierre.' Caroline was immediately enveloped in a hug. 'These are my friends.' She extricated herself from his enthusiastic embrace.

He raised his hands again. 'Ah, the beautiful ladies,' he said in heavily accented English. 'You are most welcome.'

'Hope he doesn't try that lark on me,' Barney said, backing into the shadows as Pierre proceeded to kiss all the girls.

''You know what Frenchmen are like,' Stella teased. 'Best stay where you are.'

'Not all evening I'm not,' Barney protested. 'I refuse to miss out on dinner. I can smell something cooking that's sending my taste buds into overdrive.'

'My *poulet* sauté à la Parisienne,' Pierre chimed in. 'It is cooked in a wine sauce and served with my special *pommes de terre* on a bed of *asperges* — how do you say the point?'

'Asparagus tips?' Stella guessed.

'*Oui*, that is right. Now, come along.

We need to eat. Then we celebrate.'

Pierre gestured for everyone to come in, and soon they were all crowded into a small back room that overlooked a tiny walled garden, which was crammed with barred cages.

He laughed at their surprise. 'You like my birds?'

'They're not real,' Stella said.

'I love to go to the bird market on a Sunday, but my weekdays are too busy to care for animals. Perhaps one day when I have made my fortune and can afford to retire to the south of France, then maybe I will have real birds. For now my daughter and her children make tiny models and I put them in my garden.'

'How sweet.' Caroline stroked a very realistic-looking robin. 'And what a charming idea.'

Pierre bustled around, pulling out chairs and lighting candles. 'Sit where you will. There is not much room so we will have to squash in, but we are all friends, *non*?'

Later after they had eaten Pierre's chicken and finished with a mouth-watering selection of tiny fresh fruit tarts, Pierre's friends descended on them and the party spilled over into the garden. A beautiful dark-haired girl wearing a striped jersey and leggings had brought along a guitar and she began to play and sing.

Stella leaned forward to thank her friend. 'This was a lovely idea of yours, Caroline.'

'I told you this place was special, didn't I? Way off the tourist route. I did invite Kaylee, but she and Mark had other plans. Bet they're not having half as much fun as we are.' She leaned back and raised her glass to one of Pierre's friends, who promptly looked as though he would be ready to die for her.

'Stop teasing the young men,' Stella chided her.

'Don't you know the rules?' Caroline laughed. 'It's what one does in Paris.'

'Look at the sky.' Barney pointed towards the stars pin-pricking the velvet

Parisian night. 'It seems different from home, doesn't it? A night for lovers?'

'Another visitor?' Pierre's voice boomed across the room, as there was a disturbance in the doorway.

'Now there's a man I could really throw my hat at,' Caroline purred.

Stella's smile of welcome faltered as she recognised the visitor.

24

'You might have told me,' Caroline grumbled.

'Told you what?' Stella asked.

'That you've managed to snaffle the best-looking man I've seen for ages.'

'I haven't snaffled him.'

'He kissed you on the cheek.'

'We live together.'

Caroline raised her eyebrows. 'You kept that quiet.'

'I mean,' Stella hastened to explain, 'I live with his mother. I'm her companion.'

'Make sure Kaylee doesn't get her hooks into him,' Caroline added with an arch smile. 'She's already made off with one of your exes.'

Deciding it would be too complicated to explain further, Stella dragged Rory away from Pierre, who was smiling at them with the amused tolerance the French display for lovers.

'Do you have to follow me everywhere?' she demanded.

'I'm actually under cover.'

'Stop sounding like a spy novel.'

Barney hovered by Rory's elbow. 'We're leaving. Are you coming?'

'We'll make our own way back,' Rory replied. 'And don't worry if we're not on the train tomorrow. We may be staying over.'

Stella cast him a questioning look. 'Are we?'

'Wish I could join you. I'll be in touch,' Barney said to Stella before following everyone out of the tiny restaurant.

'You do not have to go too,' Pierre insisted. 'The night is young.'

'Another time perhaps, and thank you for a lovely evening,' Stella replied.

'You are most welcome. I am very choosy about my clientele, and only those on my approved list are permitted to dine with me. I am pleased to say you are among that select number.' Pierre thrust a piece of paper into Stella's hands. 'My private telephone number, *cherie*. It is not in the book so do not lose it.'

He squeezed her fingers with a suggestive smile before opening the solid wooden door and wishing them goodnight.

'I know it goes against your feminist principles,' Rory said, 'but I think we had better walk arm in arm. You never know who's hanging around dark corners on nights like this.'

Strolling along, Stella tried to imagine what life had been like in the late nineteenth century when the area was a centre of bohemian life, and respectable Paris was scandalised by the goings on. They passed Montmartre's famous vineyard and were soon back among the busier artists' area where, despite the lateness of the hour, the cafés were still bustling.

They were now standing in front of the Sacré-Coeur.

'Where are you staying?' Stella asked Rory.

'I got a room in your hotel. Before you ask, you left the details with Doreen.'

247

'And your reason for being here?'

'I've an appointment tomorrow with an art connoisseur. He is publicity shy, that's why I'd like you to come along. My cover is that I'm a journalist looking for material. I'm sure being French he'll open up if he thinks I'm here with a female companion, enjoying a short break in Paris. So are you on for tomorrow morning?' Stella nodded. 'In that case we'd better get back. Another early start, I'm afraid.'

'The others were back ages ago,' Mark grumbled from his seat in the bar as they entered the hotel foyer. 'Where've you been?'

'For a walk,' Rory replied.

'Can I tempt you to a nightcap?'

'I'm off to bed,' Stella replied.

'Me too.' Rory joined Stella in the creaky lift.

'I suppose you don't fancy a nightcap in my room?' he suggested.

'See you at breakfast,' Stella said firmly.

'Wear comfortable shoes,' Rory called after her.

*   *   *

Their drive took them out to the west of the city. After a short burst along the autoroute, they turned down an impressive tree-lined avenue that led up to the landscaped gardens of what was originally the country residence of minor cousins of royalty.

'The property was seized during the revolution,' Rory explained. 'The family fled to England. When they returned all they managed to retain was stables, the water garden and the coach house.'

A distinguished-looking man was waiting for them outside a white building. He kissed Stella's hand. 'Welcome. I am Charles, and you are — ?'

'Stella Bates.'

'Indeed as beautiful as the stars, I think. Monsieur Loates is not your husband, unless you are *très moderne* and do not use your married name?'

'We're not married,' Stella replied firmly.

'I thought perhaps we could walk

down to the orangery.' Charles closed the door to the coach house behind him. 'My housekeeper has provided a picnic lunch. The countess is away.' With a wicked smile at Stella he added, 'But we shall manage without her. We will start. Monsieur Loates can catch up after he has parked the car. You would like that I tell you a little of the history of the park?' he asked.

Stella agreed with enthusiasm, wishing she had been allowed to bring her camera. She recognised several examples of rare plants, something she would like to have shown to Fenella.

'When my family returned from exile in your charming country, after a regrettable period in French history, the property had been badly treated. Our treasures had been seized and a beautiful collection of priceless miniatures disappeared. But the family motto is courage under adversity, and so my forebears set about putting things right, and gradually the gardens came back to life.'

'They are beautiful,' Stella admitted.

'In the summer we open to the public. We have boating on the lake and a rose arbour, a maze, and a miniature train ride for those whose feet ache.'

'Where do you keep your works of art?' Stella asked.

'I am merely the custodian. They are in the gallery, which is a grand name for a corridor. That is our great attraction. We do not keep them in a museum.' Charles paused by a long glass-domed building. 'The orangery was an innovation of one of my ancestors. He was an enthusiastic collector and travelled extensively in the Far East. He brought back many exotic plants. They need the humidity of a warm climate to survive.'

Rory had now joined them. 'Will we be allowed access to the main house?'

'It is closed for redecoration,' Charles replied, 'but I do have sketches of the more important paintings. You may borrow them for your research if you so wish.'

'I'll take great care of them,' Rory promised.

'I will help in any way I can, but I do not wish to be involved in anything as vulgar as publicity.'

'I understand.'

'My family has always guarded its privacy. My father did not even use his title, fearing it would attract attention.' He again subjected Stella to his wicked smile. 'I use it sometimes, especially with the ladies. Now, can I tempt you to a light lunch? We have grapes from our own vine, fresh figs warm from the sun, cheese from the home farm, and all manner of tarts and pastries. After lunch we will take a trip out onto the lake.'

It was warm in the orangery, and Stella's head began to ache from a combination of heat and wine.

'There is a small island in the middle where you will see the famous statue of my celebrated great-grandmother. She was an artist's muse.' Charles tapped the side of his nose with his forefinger. 'Discretion forbids me from telling you which one, but it was due to Marie's charms that we could afford to build the orangery. I will show you a painting of her. It is the only one we do not put on display. Her artist friend, I think, would have married her.' He shrugged. 'But he already had a wife.'

It was with great difficulty that Rory managed to persuade Charles that he wanted to accompany him and Stella on their trip to the island in the middle of the lake.

'Are you sure you would not prefer to sit in the sun to write up your notes?'

Charles gave in with good grace when Rory assured him he wouldn't, and the three of them made the little outing to the lake. Charles proved a well-informed host, pointing out all the attractions of the gardens and the Renaissance architecture of the rebuilt main house, visible through gaps in the trees. He also provided Rory with information regarding the works of art on permanent display in the gallery.

'Please contact me if there is anything else you wish to know,' he said as the afternoon came to an end.

'What a charming man,' Stella said.

'I can see you enjoyed his company,' Rory said.

'You wanted me to go under cover, so I acted the part.'

'You virtually had Charles eating out of your hand.'

'How about a thank-you? I've had to rearrange my plans at a moment's notice, and all you've done is grumble because a very attractive French count kissed my hand and told me I was beautiful.'

'If I went on at you like that you'd bite my head off.'

'Agreed,' Stella said, then added, 'Look out!'

Rory swerved and they received a blast on the horn from an irate motorist.

Rory gritted his teeth. 'Thank goodness we're going home tomorrow. The likes of Pierre and Charles are far too free with their favours.'

'Talking of free favours,' Stella said, 'I

need someone to carry my shopping.'

'I hate shopping,' Rory objected.

'This is Paris,' Stella insisted, 'so unless you can think up a really good excuse you're coming with me. Do you have a good excuse?' she asked.

'No, but I'm working on it,' Rory replied with a grim twist to his mouth.

25

'I've put your name down for the senior team,' Tom informed Rory over Saturday morning breakfast. He lobbed a sugar lump at him when there was no reaction.

'Tom,' Rory remonstrated with him, 'behave.'

'You're not listening,' he complained. 'They were a man short 'cos someone took a sickie. Last year the seniors were all out for fifty. It was so embarrassing.' Tom rolled his eyes at the memory. 'Even you can't do worse than that.'

'At what?' Rory looked up from his notes.

'Cricket,' everyone bellowed.

'Don't pinch all that French jam.' A tussle ensued as Tom wrestled with his sister for control of the jar. 'Stella gave it to me.'

'She said it was ours to share.'

'Whatever you want, the answer's no,' Rory said firmly.

'Don't be difficult, Rory.' Doreen folded her morning newspaper and removed her glasses. 'It will make a nice outing for everyone.'

'What will?'

'The parents versus the school cricket match. You're down to play. Haven't you been listening?'

'We thought it was a good idea,' Stella said.

Rory glared at Stella. 'Are you to blame for this?'

'Actually it was me,' Fenella piped up, licking apricot jam off the spoon.

Rory swivelled round to face his niece.

'I put Stella's name forward for the presentation photographs,' Fenella continued as though she were explaining things to a child. 'So we thought it was only fair for you to be involved in school life too. It's called helping the community.'

'I haven't played cricket for years.'

'Stop sounding petulant, Rory,' Doreen rebuked him. 'At times you're worse than the children.'

'When is this match, anyway?' he demanded.

'This afternoon.'

'What?' Rory objected. 'I can't possibly play at such short notice.'

'Nonsense,' Doreen replied. 'Look at the way you got yourself to Paris at a moment's notice.'

'That was different.'

'Only because you thought Stella had gone off with her old boyfriend.' Fenella tossed back her newly styled hair. The much nicer Fenella had replaced the sulky-faced girl of a few days ago. Stella hoped that whatever had caused the blip in her behaviour had been resolved.

'Right, that's settled,' Doreen said as Stella watched Rory redden in the face.

'My trip to Paris was for business reasons.' His jaw sounded tight as he spoke.

'Course it was,' Fenella crowed. 'That's why Stella came back with a handbag to die for and lots of scrummy eats. And don't say you didn't go shopping with her, because she told me how you grumbled about carrying all the bags.'

'As we have a busy day ahead of us,' Doreen said, raising her voice, 'I suggest everyone vacate the kitchen now.'

'Will Pamela be joining us?' Stella asked.

A look of concern crossed Doreen's face. 'She's feeling tired. Perhaps you'd look in on her later, Rory?'

'I'll join her for coffee,' Stella volunteered. 'I could tell her about Paris.'

'Don't forget you're on duty from half past two onwards,' Doreen said.

Pamela greeted Stella with a wan smile as she carried the coffee tray into her sitting room.

'How nice. Would you pour? I know I'm being dreadfully lazy, but it's lovely sitting here in the sun and I don't want to move.'

'Is your ankle still bothering you?' Stella asked.

'A little,' she admitted, 'but I mustn't burden you with my troubles. Tell me about Paris. I don't believe I've thanked you properly for the lovely scarf.'

By the time Stella had spent over an hour with Pamela, then sorted through her latest batch of photos and snatched a quick sandwich, Tom and Fenella were ready for the match.

'You drive them over, Stella,' Doreen suggested. 'Rory and I will follow on. I'll make sure the star batsman gets there on time.'

The cricket ground was seething with visitors.

'Where do I go?' Stella looked round in confusion.

'No idea,' Tom said as he shot out of the car, clutching his pads. ''Spect I'm needed at the nets.'

A clipboard-clutching teacher approached the car.

'I'm doing the teas,' Stella explained.

'Then I suggest you head for the

pavilion.' The teacher peered inside the car. 'Fenella, you're down for meeting and greeting.'

Fenella carried on texting. Stella nudged her.

'Busy,' she mumbled.

The teacher raised her eyes and looked at Stella in exasperation.

'I don't know what gets into them sometimes,' she said. She saw to her concern that the sulky look was back. 'Fenella, manners.'

'Cricket's boring,' Fenella announced. She jumped out of the car and headed towards the main school building. Stifling her annoyance, Stella parked the car, unable to shake off a sense of unease. At breakfast Fenella had been full of enthusiasm for the afternoon.

Stella caught sight of Doreen waving at her from the pavilion steps. 'Hurry up,' Doreen urged her.

A muted roar from the pitch announced the arrival of the teams.

'Who's in first?' Stella asked.

'The boys. The tea break falls between

the two innings. Let's cheer them on.'

Stella found two spare deckchairs. 'Which side are we supporting?'

'I'll do the boys, you do the parents,' Doreen said. 'Look, it's Tom,' she said with pride as two boys walked past them and onto the pitch. 'He's opening bat. Doesn't he look sweet?' She cupped her hands. 'Good luck, darling,' she called after him.

He turned a very pink face towards her as everyone laughed.

'I don't think you were supposed to do that,' Stella chided.

'Sorry, keep forgetting he's growing up. I only wanted him to know he has my full support.'

'I think he knows that already,' Stella replied with an indulgent smile. Doreen had a kind heart and, exasperating though she could be, there was no doubt she loved her family.

The afternoon sun bore down on Stella's back. 'If I fall asleep you will wake me, won't you?'

Doreen looked scandalised. 'You

can't nod off. Think of the honour of the school.' She gestured towards the pitch. 'And if that's too much effort, concentrate on the fielders, Rory's over there to the left of the wicket. I must say, he and Tom look lovely in their whites.'

Rory stood a good head taller than most of the team. His rolled-up shirtsleeves revealed his strong brown arms; and with a school tie holding up his borrowed trousers, he looked the epitome of every schoolboy's hero.

'Thank heavens I saw off that Jackie James female.' Doreen began to clap loudly as there was a loud thwack. 'Good shot. That's a six.'

'I wouldn't have thought someone as persistent as Jackie would have given up so easily,' Stella said.

'I told her you and Rory were enjoying a romantic break in Paris. Careful, you've spilt orange juice on the grass.'

'Doreen, you shouldn't go round telling people I'm Rory's latest.'

'We're trying to watch the match,' a pompous-looking man hushed Doreen.

'So am I,' Doreen bridled. 'It was my great-nephew Tom Waugh who just scored that six.'

'Congratulations, madam.' He tipped his hat at her. 'Now can we follow the rest of the match in peace?'

'His uncle — my nephew, Rory Loates — is about to go in to bowl now,' she added.

'Rory Loates? Isn't he that reporter chap? He does some fine stuff.'

'We're here to watch the match,' Doreen instructed him with a wink at Stella.

There was another cheer as one of the fielders caught the ball.

'What a shame. Rory should never have bowled Tom out like that,' said Doreen.

'He didn't catch the ball,' Stella pointed out.

'The bowler always gets the credit, even when some poor chump has run halfway across the field and performed an acrobatic manoeuvre to catch it.'

A red-faced Tom stomped back to the pavilion and glared Doreen into silence.

'Duty calls,' Doreen said as the last boy went in to bat. 'We'd better check on the urn and get the cling film off the cakes. There'll be a stampede once the innings is over.'

* * *

Stella collapsed onto a plastic seat after the last jam doughnut had been eaten and everyone had vacated the tea tent. 'Is there any tea left?'

'Enough for a wet and warm,' Doreen replied. 'And I managed to snaffle some fruit cake.'

'Have you seen Fenella anywhere?' Stella asked. 'I thought she and her friends were going to help clear away.'

'I hope she's not up to mischief,' Doreen said.

'Things are hotting up,' their gentleman neighbour informed them as they settled back in their deck chairs.

A loud burst of clapping was followed by an announcement over the tannoy that ten runs were needed for the senior team to equal the score of the juniors.

'He's out!' someone shouted as wicket and stumps collapsed.

'Rory's going in to bat now,' Doreen said as she inspected her programme.

'Someone who needs no introduction,' the commentator announced. 'Please welcome Rory Loates, ladies and gentlemen. Rory stood in at the last moment, so we're especially grateful to him.'

Rory raised his bat to acknowledge the cheerful applause. Several of the spectators stood up to clap him onto the pitch.

'Tom will want revenge,' Doreen said as Rory lined up to take the first ball.

'It's a four,' the commentator announced.

Two runs later, Rory was batting again. A fielder dropped a catch, causing widespread groans. Stella could hardly bear to look as Rory lined up at the wicket and prepared to hit the last ball of Tom's over. It soared over the boundary line.

'It's another six,' the commentator declared. 'The seniors win the day.'

'That'll teach Tom to volunteer Rory for the match,' Doreen commented as spectators raced onto the pitch to congratulate the players. 'I'd better go and console Tom. Can you find Fenella? Goodness knows where the girl has got to.'

'She's round the back of the music room,' a passing pupil informed Stella. 'You didn't hear it from me.' The look she gave Stella spoke volumes.

'Where's the music room?' Stella demanded.

The girl pointed to a square red-bricked building then scuttled away.

'You'd better get over there and see what's going on,' Doreen said.

'On my way,' Stella replied.

26

Rory strode into Stella's studio. 'They've all been suspended.'

The prints Stella had been working on slipped from her fingers. 'Including Fenella?' she gasped.

'The head said he could make no exceptions.'

'But she wasn't involved in any bullying.'

'It seems she was.'

'He's got it wrong. Fenella was being bullied. She told me the gang threatened to post things about her online, things that were untrue.'

'It's her word against theirs.'

'Fenella doesn't fib.'

'Maybe not,' Rory agreed, 'but several parents have reported their children having pocket money taken off them and other unpleasant incidents. One or two named Fenella.'

Stella felt sick. She should have realised things weren't right from Fenella's erratic behaviour.

'June and Andrew will have to be told. There's Tom to consider too.'

'He wasn't involved,' Stella said.

'When Fenella was suspended he threatened to leave. I'm sorry,' Rory apologised, 'none of this is your problem.'

'I feel as though it is,' Stella admitted. Her gaze fell to the tie Rory had used as a belt for his cricket whites. 'Congratulations, by the way. The match?' she prompted.

'Your team won.'

'Thanks. I think that's another reason why Tom is being so stroppy.' He ran a hand through his hair.

'Because his side lost?'

'That, and Fenella upsetting his big day, resulting in the pair of them being bundled off home in disgrace.'

'Where's Tom now?'

'Playing loud music in his room. I've left the pair of them to it for the moment. Give everyone a chance to cool down.' Rory looked over Stella's shoulder. 'Are these your Paris pictures?' He glanced through them. 'I like the ones of the portcullis. By the way, we ran a check on Henry Lowring. He's definitely Buttonhole Man, and his contact at the gallery was a temporary dispatch clerk.'

'I still don't see how the scam works.'

'It's a sophisticated operation. Someone comes to view and asks for a photo of the picture.'

'But the paintings I saw were only in Mr Jenkins's gallery because they were being cleaned.'

'A practised conman could easily convince someone like Mr Jenkins that they had the owner's permission to view. No disrespect intended to Mr Jenkins.'

'There was a viewing the day I took my insurance photos,' Stella remembered. 'The extra photo I took wasn't part of the insurance assessment, but an agent had been in to see it and he needed copies. I had to hurry because it began to rain, and that was why I inadvertently took Henry's photo in the first place.'

'It would seem our fraudsters have been the victims of their own scam.'

'I'm glad the mole wasn't a permanent member of Mr Jenkins's staff. He would have been mortified,' Stella said in relief as she began to clear away her things. 'Talking about photos . . . ' she began.

'I don't want you getting involved,' Rory warned her. 'It's a dangerous game these men are playing and the stakes are high. They wouldn't hesitate to deal with anybody who got in their way.'

'I'm actually back on Fenella now,' she explained.

'What about her?' Rory asked, his mouth set in a grim twist.

'Mr Wolff, her head teacher, asked me to do the photos for the summer presentation. Do you think I could use it as a bargaining tool to have Fenella reinstated on the strength of waiving my fee?'

'I couldn't possibly ask you to do that,' Rory protested.

'I've done little to earn my keep as Pamela's companion since Doreen joined us.'

'You've done more than enough in other ways.'

'I'd like to help, and I may be able to turn the situation around.'

'Either way, I do have to tell her parents.'

'Can you hold fire for a few days?' Stella asked.

'I suppose I could. I've got to fly to Scotland on Monday.'

'That should give me enough time to speak to Mr Wolff.'

'Are you sure you want to do this?'

'I wouldn't want Tom or Fenella's future to be compromised over what happened today.'

'Thank you.' Rory raised a hand as if to touch her face, then let it fall to his side.

Stella wasn't sure why she was doing this, but she knew what it was like to make a youthful mistake. Amy had put her right when she had been in a similar situation, and if she could do the same for Tom and Fenella then she was prepared to make sacrifices.

'If you're finished here,' Rory said, 'I'd like to get out of these cricket clothes and take a shower.'

The accommodation arrangements had remained unchanged since Doreen had arrived and Stella still slept in the main house, with Rory occupying the extension whenever he wasn't staying over in his flat or working away from home.

Stella stowed her laptop away. 'By the way — ' she began.

'Not more bad news?' Rory asked with a resigned look on his face.

'Doreen's told Jackie about our trip to Paris. She said we went there as a couple,' Stella added.

'That was our cover, wasn't it?' Rory's smile suggested he wasn't too perturbed by this latest piece of information.

'It was the story we gave Charles.'

'And you did agree to go through with the subterfuge, didn't you?'

'That's exactly what it was, a subterfuge. It wasn't for real, and only for the weekend visit.'

'I'd like to keep up the pretence for the moment if you don't mind.'

'Why?'

'We may need to use it again, and it worked well, didn't it? Without your help, the investigation could fall apart.'

'You're backing me into a corner,' Stella protested.

'You wouldn't want to jeopardise the inquiry, would you?'

'Of course not.'

'Then do you really mind what Doreen said about us?' Rory asked in a gentler tone of voice, adding, 'I know it's asking a lot, and that's something this family seems to be good at, but if we could pretend for a little while longer . . . ?'

'I'll be in the main house,' Stella said by way of reply. She had been outmanoeuvred and they both knew it.

'I understand what you're saying, Miss Bates,' Mr Wolff said, looking across his desk at her. 'Fenella is at an impressionable age, and I hate to admit defeat with any pupil. I wouldn't hear of you waiving your fee if I reinstate Fenella. Please hear me out,' he continued, stalling Stella's interruption. 'I wouldn't want your offer to be constituted as a bribe, so our original agreement stands.'

'I want to do the best for Fenella — and Tom too,' she replied.

Mr Wolff steepled his fingers, a thoughtful expression crossing his face. 'You know that Tom has expressed solidarity with his sister by having himself suspended?'

'Yes.'

'Have you tried to persuade him otherwise?'

'He won't discuss the matter with me.'

'Young adults can be extremely stubborn. I speak from my experience as a father, not as a teacher.' He looked down at his notes. 'I am aware of Tom and Fenella's family situation, and may I say I think you've done a splendid job.'

'I have?' Stella asked in surprise.

'I trust I'm not speaking out of turn, but the children regularly sing your praises and are looking forward to welcoming you into the family. I do hope this upset hasn't changed your relationship with Mr Loates?'

'It's not official.' Stella wished she had never agreed to be Rory's cover in Paris. The story was spreading like wildfire.

'I think it only fair to warn you it's common knowledge in the school. Rory Loates is very popular, and his programmes are always the first to be requested on nights when pupils are allowed to watch television. However, back to the problem in hand. I feel Fenella was weak-willed and easily led, but I wouldn't want her to suffer a lifelong regret for something that happened as a result of a youthful indiscretion. We've all done things which, with the benefit of hindsight, would have been better left undone.'

'Are you saying you'll take Fenella back?'

'I'm keen to encourage her interest in horticulture and I have appointed a lady gardener for the summer term. If you can assure me that Fenella will attend all her lectures and do community work in her spare time, I'm prepared to agree to your request.'

'What about the others?' Stella asked. When Stella had caught them behind the music room, they were about to relieve a rather plump girl of her bag of doughnuts and the pocket money her parents had given her to spend at the cricket match.

'The ringleader, a girl called Gloria, has been relocated to a progressive school more suited to her character. Another was due to leave at the end of term, and the third is moving to Australia with her family. So as that only leaves Fenella, I think we can safely reinstate her.'

'Thank you, Mr Wolff. You don't

know how grateful I am.'

'You may not feel quite so relieved when I discuss the question of Tom.'

'You'll be taking him back too?'

'Cricket is all very well, but recreational activities must not override his studies. I have been informed that Tom regularly skips lessons to indulge in his passion for batting. His mid-year exam results were poor. In fact he was placed in the bottom third of his class. Letters to his grandmother go unanswered — due, I suspect, to Tom not passing them on.'

'I had no idea,' Stella apologised.

'This business with Fenella may have been the excuse he was looking for to wriggle out of things. What I propose is if you can get both children to promise on their honour that things will improve, I am prepared to have them back. I should really be speaking to a member of the family on matters as important as these, but in the circumstances perhaps this is the best course of action to take.'

'Rory — Mr Loates — is away, but

he will be telephoning his sister when he gets back. The children's grandmother would have come with me today, but she has mobility problems.'

Mr Wolff stood up to shake hands. 'In that case I look forward to welcoming the children back, and I hope to see you at the presentation ceremony in the summer.'

Outside in the car park Stella let her shoulders sag with relief. Briefly dialling Doreen's number, she updated her on events.

'Brilliant. Knew you could do it,' she enthused. 'Who'd have children?' She sighed. 'I had no idea they could be so devious. Do you want me to break the news?'

'I think it might be better coming from me.'

'You're probably right,' Doreen agreed. 'I wouldn't want to put my foot in it. What are you up to now?'

'I have to do my deliveries.' Stella looked at the pile of work on her passenger seat. 'I'll be home about six.'

'I'll make sure they're on parade,' Doreen promised.

★ ★ ★

Fenella hugged Stella when she explained the terms of her reinstatement.

'Promise you won't let me down again?' Stella looked searchingly into the girl's brown eyes.

'I won't,' she agreed fervently and danced a little jig on the carpet. 'My own garden.'

'Mr Wolff didn't exactly say that,' Stella said in an effort to curb her enthusiasm.

Fenella stopped dancing. 'You won't be too hard on Tom, will you? He only did it for me.'

To Stella's surprise, Tom was less than accommodating.

'I don't care about exams.' He tilted his chin in challenge. 'What good are they?'

Stella recognised the signs of adolescent bravado. 'They'll help you get on in life.'

'Says who?'

'They may not seem important now, Tom.' She held back the urge to brush his hair off his forehead. 'But one day you'll understand.'

'No I won't.' He crossed his arms in an uncompromising stance.

'Fenella's going back to school next week. Don't you want to join her?'

'I'm going for a ride on my bike.' Tom leapt off his bed and ran out of the room.

'Don't be too late,' Stella called out. Moments later she heard the squeak of bicycle spokes.

★ ★ ★

When Tom had not returned by suppertime, Stella began to get worried. 'Have you any idea where he could have gone?' she asked Fenella. The girl shrugged.

'Have you tried Hammonds Farm?' Pamela suggested. 'I know he goes there sometimes.'

281

'What's the number?' Stella picked up the phone.

'I don't know,' Pamela admitted.

'Fenella? Do you know it?' Stella demanded.

The girl's look of unease deepened.

'Out with it,' Doreen ordered. 'I've had enough of this nonsense.'

'Tom's got a girlfriend,' she admitted.

'He's only twelve,' Stella protested.

Doreen silenced her with a look. 'When does he visit this girlfriend?'

'It's Cheryl,' she admitted. 'The girl with the bag of doughnuts? She lives on the farm.'

'We still don't know if that's where Tom has gone,' Pamela put in.

'I'm calling the police,' Doreen announced.

'Let me go down the farm first and check,' Stella suggested.

Doreen grabbed the receiver. 'Tom may be lying injured in the middle of nowhere.'

Pamela held up a hand. 'Isn't that a vehicle outside?'

Headlights lit up the sitting room. Stella snatched back the sitting room curtains.

Doreen peered over her shoulder. 'Who do we know with a muddy four-by-four?'

27

Doreen was the first to reach the Land Rover. 'Where've you been, you little tinker?' She grabbed Tom by his shoulders as he tried to get out. 'What's this about a girlfriend?' The next moment, despite Tom's protests, she hugged him hard.

A ruddy-faced man stepped forward. 'Lady Loates?'

'Who are you?' Doreen looked him up and down. 'For your information it's Miss Soames, and if anything's happened to my great-nephew you won't hear the last of this.'

'Doreen,' Tom protested, 'let go of me.'

'Perhaps we should all go inside,' Stella suggested before things got out of hand.

'You're in trouble,' Fenella crowed as a shamefaced Tom shuffled towards the house.

'You told them,' he accused her.

'What if I did?'

'I trusted you. I don't want to talk to anyone, ever again.' Tom stuck out his lower lip and stomped into the kitchen.

Doreen followed. 'None of your tantrums now. Remember, you are in disgrace. Going off like that without a word to anyone — what were you thinking of?'

'You're not my mother,' Tom retaliated. 'I can do what I like.'

'Doreen,' Stella stepped in, 'will you take this gentleman — I'm sorry, I didn't catch your name.'

'Phil Wright. I live at Hammonds Farm, down the foot of the hill.'

'Will you take Mr Wright into the sitting room and introduce him to Lady Loates?'

'I can't stay long, I'm afraid,' he said with a pleasant smile. 'I've left the vet to deal with things in my absence, but I'd like to get back as soon as I can.' He turned to Doreen. 'I did ask my wife to telephone you to tell you Tom had been with us, but it was only after we left that I realised she didn't know the number. It was my fault you've been so worried about him. I do apologise.'

'Come through,' a slightly mollified Doreen invited. 'You can update my sister and me as to what's been going on. Stella, can you talk to Tom? Fenella, perhaps you'd care to join us in the sitting room?'

Fenella crossed her arms and stood by the side of her brother. 'I'm staying here with Tom.'

'I can't allow that,' Doreen began to protest, but she saw the stubborn expression on Fenella's face and gave in. 'Oh, very well. I'll speak to the pair of you later.'

'Why don't we sit down?' Stella drew out kitchen chairs for them all. 'Would anyone like a drink?' she asked.

Both youngsters shook their heads. Sparky whined and, sensing the tension in the air, laid her head on Tom's knee. Stella noticed the boy's eyes were over-bright as his resistance began to crumble. The kitchen clock ticked comfortingly in the background against the hum of the fridge.

'Are you hungry?' Stella asked.

Again Tom shook his head.

Fenella was the first to tackle him. 'You should be. It's your fault we haven't had any supper, and Stella cooked your favourite — three-cheese lasagne, with strawberry ripple ice cream for afters.'

'Fenella, please.' Stella put a warning hand on her arm.

'Sorry,' Tom murmured in a small voice.

Fenella wrinkled her nose. 'You smell of cows. Where have you been?'

'In Mr Wright's cow shed.'

'What were you doing there?' Stella kept her voice gently neutral. Tom didn't appear to have suffered any lasting effects from his adventure, but she didn't want to make any hasty decisions before she was in full possession of the facts.

'Nothing,' Tom replied.

'Don't fib. You were with Cheryl,' Fenella accused.

'So what if I was?'

'Mr Wright's daughter?' Fenella filled in for Stella's benefit. 'She's a fat girl in Tom's class.'

'She is not fat!' Tom shouted back at her. 'She's nice and kind and gentle.'

'I won't warn you again, Fenella,' Stella said sternly. She looked back at Tom. 'Now, exactly what were you doing in the cow shed with Cheryl?'

'We were keeping each other company.'

Whatever Tom had been up to, Stella knew it would do no good shouting at him.

Fenella leaned forward, an excited look on her face. 'Bet *I* know what you were up to.'

Tom threw her a look of scorn before saying, 'The cows,' then lowered his eyes and continued to stroke Sparky's head.

'What about them?' Stella coaxed.

'We watched them and we talked.'

'I see.'

'One of them is in calf,' Tom explained. 'They think it might be twins and she was uncomfortable.'

'You stayed with the cows all the time while you were talking to Cheryl?'

'She listens to me. We're friends.' He glanced nervously at his sister. 'You're not to say unkind things about her.'

Fenella's face was now alight with interest. 'Did you see the baby calf being born?'

'Mr Wright came in with the vet and found us. They wouldn't let us stay. I wanted to help. I want to be a vet when I grow up, then I can look after animals in pain.'

'In that case,' Stella spoke steadily, 'wouldn't it be a good idea to start studying for your exams?'

'Might be,' Tom acknowledged. 'But what about cricket?'

'You can play cricket as well, but if you really want to look after animals then you're going to have to buckle down and work. Animals trust us, Tom, and if you want to earn their trust then you have to work at it.'

'Stella's right,' Fenella agreed. 'Think what might have happened to that cow if the vet hadn't done his training.'

Stella threw her a grateful look.

'It was brilliant in the cow shed. Cheryl was telling me she goes down there a lot because people make horrid remarks about her. Your friends do it all the time.' He looked at Fenella, who blushed. 'And they've posted horrid things about her on a website.'

'They're not coming back,' Fenella said. 'Mr Wolff told Stella they've gone.'

'Really?' Tom looked hopefully at Stella.

'Really.' She smiled at him.

'Can I tell Cheryl?'

'Later.'

'You've been to see Mr Wolff?' Tom's voice was shaky again.

'I have.'

'What did he say about me?' Tom asked.

'He expressed disappointment in your mid-term exam results,' Stella replied. 'He feels you let him down.'

Tom blinked. 'I was unhappy,' he confessed.

'We all feel unhappy at times, but we don't run away,' Fenella said.

'You did. You didn't help out at the cricket match and you said you would.'

'Mr Wolff,' Stella cut in, 'also said he hoped you would reconsider your decision not to return to school, Tom. I gave him my word that you would. You're not going to let me down, are you?' Again Stella held her breath, hoping Tom would accept the lifeline she had thrown him.

'I'll go back if Fenella comes with me,' he said in a quavery voice.

'I already have her word,' Stella assured him. 'Fenella?'

The girl gave a quick nod. 'I've been promised my own garden. You can help me weed it.'

Tom reacted with a hint of his old spirit. 'Yuck! Who wants to dig around in wet earth looking for worms?'

'It's better than clearing out smelly hamster cages.'

'What I suggest is,' Stella butted in, 'that you thank Mr Wright for bringing you home, Tom, and apologise for all the trouble you've caused him and his wife. Then perhaps we can invite Cheryl up to tea one day.' She kicked Fenella's foot under the table and gave her a warning glance as a protest hovered on the girl's lips. 'You could show her how to do her hair, Fenella, or lend her some of the make-up your mother bought you.'

'She's my friend,' Tom protested, 'and she doesn't like girly things.'

'I expect she'd like a new friend though, don't you?'

'Might do,' Tom conceded.

'And you'll go back to school with Fenella?'

Tom nodded.

'I think you've made a wise decision, Tom.' His face glowed under Stella's praise. 'Let's hope it's the first of many.

Now is there anything else you want to get off your chest?'

'Can I have something to eat?' he asked. 'I'm starving.'

'The cheese on the lasagne will have gone all chewy by now,' Fenella grumbled.

'In that case you can exercise your cooking skills and make us some beans on toast, can't you?'

Something in the tone of Stella's voice warned the pair of them she meant business. Without further protest, they leapt to their feet and began arguing about who was going to set the table.

★   ★   ★

Rory arrived just as Mr Wright was leaving. 'So Tom wants to be a vet now? Hope he doesn't change his mind next week.'

'I think it's more than a passing fancy. He is a gentle boy and he was very good when Sparky was ill.'

'It's too late to call June.' Rory opened a bottle of wine. 'Care to join me?' he asked Stella.

'How did your trip go?' she asked.

'Important people are starting to sit up and take notice. We may have to hand over our files again.'

'After all your hard work?'

'It's a hazard of the job, but we don't seek the limelight. We expose injustices and bring them to public notice.' Rory paused. 'I'm glad Henry's threats came to nothing.'

Stella leaned back on the sofa and closed her eyes. Now everyone else was in bed, the house had settled down for the night. She felt Rory's weight shift beside her.

'You were snoring,' he teased.

Pamela's carriage clock chimed the half hour.

'Bed for you, I think,' he said.

'What about you?'

'I've a couple of reports I need to write up before I turn in.'

Still only half-awake, Stella lost her

footing and stumbled against Rory. Before she realised his intention, she was in his arms and his lips were on hers.

28

'I couldn't resist it,' Rory confessed. 'You looked so vulnerable when you were asleep.' Stella wriggled free from his embrace. 'See you in the morning.'

'Stella?' A pyjama-clad figure was waiting for her on the landing.

Tom's kiss as he rushed into her arms lacked the passion of Rory's embrace, but Stella responded with enthusiasm.

'I really do want to do well in my exams. Will you help me?'

'We'll help each other,' she promised, stroking down his hair. 'Now you've had a busy day, so off to bed with you.'

She knocked gently on Fenella's door. 'Are you asleep?' She poked her head into the room.

Fenella yanked off her earphones. 'Not yet. You can come in.' She made space for Stella on the edge of her bed.

'You're happy about going back to

school?' Stella asked.

Fenella nodded. 'Do I have to have chubby Cheryl over for tea?' she asked plaintively.

'You do,' Stella said firmly. 'Think how you felt when you were being bullied.'

''S'pose you're right,' Fenella agreed, then brightened up as she said, 'Actually, being a farmer's daughter, she might know about plants and stuff.'

'That's something you can talk about together, can't you?'

Fenella snuggled down and Stella turned out the light. Hearing the murmur of voices from the room Doreen and Pamela shared, Stella decided not to disturb them.

★　★　★

'Telephone for you,' Doreen called up the stairs the next morning. 'Mr Jenkins wants to know if you would be free to call by some time.'

Stella decided to visit him first, then plan the rest of her day accordingly. She spotted a car sporting French number plates parked across the entrance to the gallery as she drove in.

'I didn't expect you quite so soon.' Mr Jenkins began searching through his files. 'I have one or two more works I would like you to photograph. By the way . . . ' He paused. 'You remember that chat we had about art fraud?'

Stella's interest was piqued. 'Yes?'

'I have a Frenchman here now talking to some of my men. He's on a fact-finding mission on the very subject. Ah, here he is,' Mr Jenkins looked over her shoulder as a newcomer entered his office.

Charles moved forward and, raising his hand to her lips, kissed it. 'The enchanting Stella.'

'You two obviously need no introduction from me. I'll leave you to catch up. I'll be in the main office,' Mr Jenkins made his excuses.

'Did you enjoy the rest of your weekend?' Charles asked. 'I hope you did some shopping on our famous Champs-Élysées.'

'We did go shopping and we had a good time, thank you,' Stella glossed over her explanation. 'But I'm holding you up.' She was anxious to deflect his interest in her relationship with Rory.

'Not at all. I was interested to see the work here,' Charles explained, not missing a beat. 'A contact of mine mentioned the gallery and suggested I visit the next time I was in England.'

Stella began to harbour another suspicion. With unfettered access to the château, Charles was in an excellent position to show off the family art collection, including the picture of his notorious ancestor Marie. No one would suspect a thing if he removed the occasional painting. He could always say he was borrowing it to show to a business client.

Another thought niggled Stella's mind. Doreen had mentioned that Henry Lowring was half French. Was Henry the contact who had mentioned Mr Jenkins's gallery?

'Have I said something to disturb you?' Charles asked.

'Not at all.' She smiled. 'But you must forgive me; I have a busy day.'

'Are you too busy to have dinner tonight?'

'I would like to meet the countess,' Stella replied.

'Alas, my wife did not accompany me.'

'What about Rory?' Stella was uneasy about accepting Charles's invitation.

'By all means, invite him if you wish.'

Doreen answered the call. 'Sorry, Stella, he's not here.'

Stella hesitated, then made her decision. 'I may be late back, Doreen. I've bumped into a friend and he suggested we have dinner together.'

'It will do you good to get away from everybody for a while.'

Charles was back by her side. 'You have finished your call?'

'Rory's out. I've left a message.'

'Then I will make a reservation for the two of us.'

Mr Jenkins popped his head round the door. 'Are you ready?' he asked.

'Coming. Sorry,' Stella apologised.

Mr Jenkins drew her out of Charles's earshot. 'I couldn't help hearing him inviting you out to dinner tonight. You do know he is married?'

'Yes I do.'

'The French do these things differently, but a word of caution might be advisable where Charles is concerned.' Mr Jenkins looked thoughtful. 'Shall we say, I wouldn't totally believe everything he says.'

'I'll bear your words in mind,' Stella promised.

'Then I'll say no more, especially as Charles is heading our way.'

'It is booked for tonight, eight o'clock,' Charles said.

★   ★   ★

'Dinner with a French count.' Fenella sat on Stella's bed with a dreamy sigh and watched her get ready. 'What's he like?'

'It's a business dinner.' Stella inspected her reflection in her mirror and applied some lipstick.

'Wish you weren't going out,' Fenella grumbled. 'Tom's gone to visit Cheryl, and Doreen and Nan are watching TV.'

'Then it might be a good opportunity for you to read up on your horticultural notes.'

'S'pose so,' Fenella agreed. Then, to Stella's surprise, the girl kissed her on the cheek. 'Don't be late, will you?'

'I'll look in before I go to bed,' she promised.

'Rory rang but I didn't tell him you were going out to dinner,' Doreen confided.

'I wouldn't have minded if you had,' Stella insisted.

'Don't be late.'

Her words were an echo of Fenella's, leaving Stella to wonder exactly what everyone thought she would be getting up to over dinner.

Charles was seated at their table by the time Stella arrived. 'I got held up. I'm sorry you were kept waiting,' she apologised.

He greeted her with a kiss on each

cheek. 'I was beginning to wonder what had happened to you. What would you like to drink?' he asked.

'I'm driving.'

'Then we will limit our consumption to one glass of wine. Shall I choose?'

Charles proved an entertaining companion, telling her of his exploits as a young man on the fringe of French high society. 'A single man is always a useful asset at dinner parties,' he added with a deprecating smile, 'especially when he is of the nobility. France is a republic and proud of it, but at the mention of a title some of its citizens forgo their principles. All they can see is a rise up the social scale.'

'Where did you meet your wife?' Stella asked.

Charles took a sip of his black coffee, which had been served in miniscule cups. He and Stella were now seated in the conservatory watching the sunset through the huge glass doors, closed against the chill of the evening.

'We grew up together. Her father was

a successful wealthy industrialist.' He shrugged. 'It is how things are done.'

Stella understood. His family was poor but titled. His wife's family had money. 'Do you have children?'

'Sadly we were not blessed, but I have a cousin who will inherit the title. He has three sons, so the line is assured.'

Stella took a deep breath. 'I think we have a mutual friend,' she began.

'We do?' Charles registered surprise.

'Henry Lowring.'

Charles paused a fraction too long before saying, 'Why would you think I am friends with Monsieur Lowring?'

'He's half French and he moves in the art world. I thought perhaps your paths might have crossed.'

'What exactly does he do?'

'He's an agent,' Stella improvised.

'I may have met him. I cannot be sure.' Charles no longer looked so relaxed.

'He wears a white rose in his buttonhole.'

This time there was no mistaking the unease in Charles's eyes. 'Have you finished your coffee?' He glanced at his watch. 'I hate to rush you, only I do have an important appointment in the morning that I am anxious not to miss. Charming though your company is, I would hate to oversleep.'

'I should be getting back too,' Stella replied. Mention of Henry Lowring had obviously struck a nerve.

Charles signalled to a waiter. 'Our coats, please.' He turned to Stella. 'It's been a lovely evening.' Now back on safe ground, he was his normal charming self. 'We must do this again some time.'

'I shall look forward to it,' Stella replied, equally insincerely.

Several lights were on as she drove into the courtyard of Minster House. She searched through her bag for the little box of sugared almonds the waiter had slipped her as a parting present. Fenella could share them with Tom.

'You're back, then.'

Stella could tell by the expression on Rory's face that it wasn't good news.

29

'There was a telephone call for you earlier,' Rory said, 'from Charles. He was telephoning to find out why you were delayed.'

'Did you tell him I'd been held up?'

'No one took the call,' Rory replied. 'They couldn't reach it in time before the answer phone cut in.'

'Well, thank you for passing the message on.'

'My mother made an attempt to answer the telephone,' Rory carried on.

A voice behind her made Stella jump. Tom poked his head round the kitchen door. 'Stella, you'll never guess what.'

'Go to bed, Tom,' Rory ordered him.

'Why?' he asked.

'Because I say so.'

'I want to tell Stella what happened.'

'Now,' Rory insisted.

Pulling a face at Stella, Tom took a

chocolate biscuit out of the tin, then did as he was told.

'There was no need to speak to Tom like that.'

The expression on Rory's face was giving nothing away. 'As I was saying, my mother tried to answer the telephone but she lost her footing. Hearing the commotion, Doreen rushed out of the sitting room to find my mother in a crumpled heap at the bottom of the stairs.'

'What?'

'Luckily Doreen had the presence of mind not to move her. It was also fortunate I chose that moment to arrive home. Doreen went to the hospital with my mother and I stayed here to look after Fenella and Tom.'

'How is Pamela?' Stella's throat was sandpaper-dry as she asked the question.

'She was lucky not to break her leg,' Rory admitted grudgingly. 'It's severely bruised and she's being kept in overnight for observation. Doreen's on her way back from the hospital.'

'I'm sorry I wasn't here.'

'If you had been, none of this would have happened.'

Stella raised her voice in indignation. 'That's an unfair thing to say.'

'I don't think so.'

'You may be able to use that tone of voice on Tom, but it won't work on me,' she retaliated. Something soft tickled her toes and she looked down to see a silky head at her feet. 'Sorry, Sparky,' she apologised to the dog. 'You don't like raised voices, do you?'

'Neither do I.' It was Fenella who now poked her head around the kitchen door. 'Is this a private fight or can anyone join in?' she asked.

'According to Rory it was my fault your grandmother fell down the stairs.'

Fenella glared at Rory. 'That's rubbish.'

Rory glared back. 'When I want your opinion, I'll ask for it.'

'Whether you want it or not, you're going to get it.' Two bright red spots of colour stained Fenella's cheeks. 'It was Nan's choice to answer the telephone. No way is Stella to blame, and it's mean of you to suggest it is.'

'Two against one.' Stella crossed her arms. 'Three,' she added as Sparky gave an urgent lick to her toes.

'You owe Stella an apology,' Fenella insisted. 'I told her not to be late back and she isn't.'

The ghost of a laugh began to bubble up in Stella's chest. Fenella was acting as though she were the mother of an errant teenage daughter. Rory looked from Fenella back to Stella just as Stella caught a wink from Fenella.

'I almost forgot. I brought these back for you and Tom.' Stella produced the little box of sugared almonds.

Fenella's face lit up. 'Brilliant.'

'They're not good for the teeth,' Rory snapped.

'Then it's just as well Stella isn't offering them to you, isn't it?' Fenella snatched the box from Stella before Rory could intervene. 'Cheers, Stella.

Nice one. I'm off to bed. Keep the noise down.' With all the dignity of her fifteen years, Fenella swept from the room.

Her exit was too much for Stella, who burst into relieved laughter. 'That told you,' she said to Rory.

'I'm glad you find the situation amusing.'

Doreen bustled through the back door. 'What on earth is going on? I had to assure the taxi driver that a murder wasn't being committed on the premises. Really, I sometimes despair of this family.'

'Stella isn't part of the family,' Rory replied. 'And I've been updating her on what's been going on while she's been out on the tiles.'

'Stop sounding like a stuffed shirt,' was Doreen's pithy response. 'Who wants to hear about Pamela?'

'I'm sorry I wasn't here, Doreen.' Now she was no longer the target of accusation, the apology fell easily from Stella's lips.

'I don't know what my nephew has been saying to you, but I can guess he wasn't asking you if you had a good time. Did you, by the way?' Doreen asked.

'Yes, thank you.'

'Good.'

'How is my mother?' Rory butted in.

'Groggy and annoyed with herself for causing such a fuss. She told the doctors she's frustrated because her ankle isn't healing, and sometimes she takes risks. Unfortunately, tonight it had consequences. Now, I've earned a hot bath then bed. Rory, if I hear that you have been bullying Stella, then I shall tell your mother. Do you understand?'

'Are all my family on your side?' Rory demanded as yet another dramatic exit was made from the kitchen.

'I don't know, but they're lovely, aren't they?'

'That's not what I'd call them.' He snatched up the jug kettle. 'Tea?' he asked over his shoulder. 'Or will it keep you awake?'

'Not if it's herbal.'

Rory peered into various containers. 'Peppermint?'

'That should aid your digestion. It might also lighten your mood.'

'I don't have anything to digest. Unlike some, I haven't had any supper.' He began sawing at a loaf of bread, then hacked off a chunk of cheese before making the tea and pouring out two mugs. 'So . . . Charles,' he prompted as he joined her at the table. 'You'd better tell me all that happened.'

'Why?' Stella replied.

'I can't think of any reason why you should,' Rory admitted with a shame-faced smile. 'I am totally in the wrong. I shouldn't have blamed you for my mother's accident. I had no right to come down on you so heavily, and yes I was put out that I'd missed the chance of having dinner with Charles. Will that do?' he asked. 'Or do I have to grovel some more?'

The clock ticked in the background against Sparky's snores. The stairs creaked, and through the open window Stella heard an owl hooting in the copse.

'I accept your apology.'

'For a moment there I thought you were going to put me through my paces a second time.' Rory smeared butter over his of bread and undid the lid on the pickle jar.

'I bumped into Charles in Mr Jenkins's gallery. According to Mr Jenkins, he was fact-finding. Charles invited me out to dinner. You were included in the invitation but you weren't here, so I went on my own.'

'Did you discover anything of interest?'

'I asked Charles if he knew Henry Lowring.'

Rory leaned forward. 'And?'

'He said he wasn't sure, but when I mentioned Henry's buttonhole his expression changed.'

Rory chewed thoughtfully. 'I suppose Charles is in a perfect position to access the family art collection.'

'If he is involved, why would he invite you to his home on the pretext of an interview?'

'Charles is no fool. He probably wanted to get in first to allay our suspicions.'

'So he invited me out tonight to see if I knew anything?'

'Can you think of any other reason?' A smile tugged the corners of Rory's mouth.

'Thanks a bunch,' Stella bridled.

'By the way, don't get any ideas. He is a married man.'

'As everyone seems keen to point out.'

'Are you seeing him again?'

'After I mentioned Henry he couldn't wait to get rid of me. I've never drunk a cup of coffee so quickly in my life.'

'Fenella and Tom were looking out the window for you, you know.'

'What on earth did they think was going to happen to me?' Stella demanded.

'Fenella was weaving a romantic fantasy about you and a French lover.'

'That's nonsense.'

'She had Tom believing it.'

'I'll go and put her right.'

'Leave her to her sugared almonds,' Rory replied. 'If she thinks we believe her story she'll start suspecting things.'

'What are we going to do about your mother?' Stella asked.

'I suggest we take one day at a time.'

The telephone began ringing in the hall.

'Now what?' Rory leapt to his feet.

Stella hovered by his shoulder.

'It's a bad line,' he said.

'Do you think it could be Charles?' Stella asked.

'Yes?' Rory's attention was diverted back to the call. '*Sí*,' he replied. 'She's here.' he thrust the telephone at Stella. 'Spain.'

'Stella? Thank goodness. I've been trying to get through to you for ages but the line's been down. It's Jennifer.' Amy's voice faded before she was cut off.

30

'Can you come out?' Amy pleaded down the telephone line when, after an agonising hour's wait, the link to Spain was reconnected. 'Jennifer went into labour early.'

Rory managed to obtain the last seat on a flight leaving the next morning, then after a few hours' sleep he had driven Stella to the airport.

'You will explain what's happened to Pamela and Doreen, won't you?' Stella asked as her flight flashed up on the departure screen.

'Yes.' Rory nudged her towards passport control. 'Hurry up before your flight closes.'

Stella had slept for most of the journey, only waking when the aircraft touched down.

The air smelt of scorched earth, pinewoods and wild olives, and the jewelled brilliance of the sky made Stella's eyes ache as she drove along. She overtook a donkey and cart, then followed a procession of vehicles loaded with fresh flowers, fish, fruit, cheeses and olives. In the distance she could hear the blast of a police whistle directing the market-day traffic.

Eventually Stella crossed over the bridge that met up with the winding cobbled street leading down to the coast. Amy had assured her that all was well with Jennifer and baby Blanche, but that didn't stop Stella worrying.

The age gap between the two girls meant they hadn't grown up together. By the time Amy married Jim, Jennifer was twenty-seven years old and Stella only eleven. Along with her two elder brothers, Jennifer had been somewhat of a stranger to Stella.

Stella swung the car down the dusty track leading to her grandfather's villa. There was none of the Moorish grandeur of the region here. It was all boat repair yards, small cafés and a few shops selling basic essentials.

'The address is Calle de la Luz,' Amy had explained. 'Ours is the peach-coloured villa.'

Stella slammed on the brakes as a figure leapt out in front of her. Instantly recognising the gangly figure and shock of snow-white hair, she returned her grandfather's vigorous wave.

He gestured towards a split-level villa. 'You can park under the lemon tree.'

Moments later she was enveloped in a bear hug. 'Welcome to Spain. You're too pale.' Her grandfather's blue eyes were full of criticism.

'And you're more weather-beaten than ever,' Stella retaliated.

'Amy's left us some fruit juice and nibbles.' Jim scooped up her suitcase. 'Follow me.'

It was cool inside the villa and Jim led her into a comfortable sitting room. Moving some magazines off a chair, he indicated that Stella should sit down.

'How's Jennifer?' she demanded.

'The baby is small but she's coming

along fine. So is Jenny. I'm sure Amy will explain everything to you.' His voice was gruff as he continued. 'I said it wasn't necessary to drag you out here, but it's good to see you. Amy's been tied up with Jennifer and I've been left to my own devices. It's been lonely of an evening not having anyone to talk to. I've given up trying to teach the locals how to play darts. They don't understand the intricacies of double top,' he explained.

'It's probably lost in the translation,' Stella said with a smile.

'I'll have you know my Spanish is coming along well,' Jim insisted. 'I was left in charge of the boatyard for a whole day last week.'

'How are things, really?' Stella bit into a sandwich.

'I'd be the first to admit it's been tough. We started off staying with Jenny and Max but obviously it wasn't a permanent arrangement. Then we lost a couple of places because we didn't understand exactly what was involved.

The owner's putting this place up for sale and we can't afford to buy it.' Jim straightened his shoulders. 'Still, I've never been one to give up.'

'You've got the cottage if you want to come back.'

'That's something else I want to talk to you about,' Jim admitted, adding, 'but not now. Let's go and introduce you to Blanche.'

As Stella walked down the cool corridors, a welcome relief from the blazing sun outside, she glimpsed proud parents in some of the side rooms, huddled around tiny bundles wrapped in soft blankets. Every so often a pink fist would emerge to coos of delight.

'It's through there,' Jim explained as they reached a set of imposing double doors.

'Aren't you coming in?'

'I ought to be getting back to work. The siesta hour is over.'

'Surely you're allowed time off?' Stella protested.

'I expect I would be if I asked for it.'

Jim gave a shamefaced smile. 'But there's nothing I can do here, and men are better off out of the way.' He kissed her on the cheek. 'See you tonight.'

Amy rose to greet her as she pushed open the double doors. 'Darling, it was so good of you to come. Baby Blanche is in the premature baby unit — she's doing well — and Jennifer here is keen to see you.'

Jennifer was sitting up in bed, flushed but happy. She held out her arms to Stella. 'I'm so glad you're here,' she said as they embraced. 'It's been ages.'

'Congratulations.' Stella smiled and produced a crocheted shawl Rory had thrust at her with embarrassment. 'It belonged to me and June. Best not go empty-handed,' he had said.

Jenny admired the delicate stitching. 'I shall save it for special occasions.' She cuddled the soft wool to her cheek.

'Why don't I go grab a coffee,' Amy suggested, 'and leave you to catch up.'

'How are you?' Stella drew up a chair. 'Much better now.' Jennifer leaned back against her pillows. 'It's Mum I'm worried about.'

'Why?'

'She hasn't left my side. She'll wear herself out. Can you take her back to the villa?'

'When have you known your mother to do anything she doesn't want to?'

'Point taken,' Jennifer laughed. 'I've tried telling her she doesn't need to stay on, but she doesn't take any notice of me.'

'I'll give it a go.'

'I have rather messed things up, haven't I?'

'A new baby in the family is a good thing. What relationship am I to baby Blanche?'

'When you work it out, let me know.' Jennifer closed her eyes.

'You're tired. I'll take Amy home and leave you to rest.'

'Give Blanche a wave for me when you see her.'

Stella found Amy in the café. 'They can't make tea here,' Amy said, 'but the coffee's delicious. They do delicious cakes too. Let's treat ourselves, then I'll take you over to the premature baby unit.'

★ ★ ★

'She's so small,' Stella said, peering through the glass.

Amy's voice was husky. 'We come from tough stock. She'll pull through.'

'I hope the new arrival isn't going to replace me in your affections.' Stella squeezed her fingers.

Her teasing produced the desired effect. 'Surely you're not jealous of a little mite like Blanche?' Amy was back to her old self.

'I shall probably spoil her as much as everyone else. Now, I've been told in no uncertain terms by your daughter that you are to get a good night's sleep, so let's go.'

Amy slipped a trusting hand into Stella's, a role reversal of responsibility that brought a lump to Stella's throat. 'I'm so glad you came,' she said.

31

Stella sat on the terrace admiring the purple bougainvillea growing up the wall of the outhouse. Even though it was early in the morning, the temperature was rising. No one else was up and she needed to get her head round all that happened.

Things weren't right between Amy and Jim. After supper he had left Amy and Stella to finish their coffee, and he hadn't returned by the time they'd gone to bed.

Stella's mobile bleeped. 'Everything's fine,' she said before Rory could start asking questions. 'Jennifer and the baby are still in hospital, but there's no cause for concern. What about Pamela?'

'She's had words with Doreen, who is threatening to decamp back to Scotland.'

Stella closed her eyes in exasperation.

'I know.' Rory's voice was full of tolerant amusement. 'It's always like this when the pair of them get together.'

'I'm not sure when I can come back.'

'Everything's under control,' Rory assured her. 'Tom and Fenella are at school. June telephoned last night. She and Andrew are thinking of returning home.'

'Then I shall have to find somewhere to live. They'll need the extension.'

'Let's cross that bridge when we come to it,' Rory was quick to reply. 'By the way, there have been two calls for you. Mr Wolff rang — nothing urgent.'

'And the other one?'

'Your agent, Mr Skinner. That one did sound more pressing.'

Hearing movement, Stella turned to see Amy standing by the double doors. 'I've got to go,' she said.

Amy was looking less drawn in the face, but her eyes were tired. 'I don't think I thanked you properly for dropping everything at a moment's notice to fly out,' she said, and tried to smile.

Stella leaned forward. 'Amy, what's wrong?'

Amy looked away.

'Where's Granddad?'

'Down the boatyard. They've got a rush job on.'

'Rory tells me Mr Skinner has been trying to get in touch.'

'We've decided to sell the cottage,' Amy admitted, still not looking Stella full in the eye.

'Is that what the trouble's about? I noticed the atmosphere last night.'

'Jim's not sure he wants to settle here permanently.'

'He was all for it in the beginning,' Stella said.

'He enjoys his work, and we've made new friends, but he feels we ought to have a base in England in case things don't work out. After that business with those rogue tenants, I told him it wasn't fair to put responsibility of that nature on your shoulders.'

'I don't mind,' Stella insisted.

'There's also the question of capital.

To put it bluntly, we need the money. I've seen a villa I like, but we can't enter into negotiations until we know the state of our finances.'

'Rory tells me Mr Skinner has been trying to get in touch with me.'

Amy swirled the last of her orange juice around in her glass, then drank it down before replying. 'I'd like you to do the sales liaison. I was going to suggest you visit us because it's not the sort of thing you can discuss over the telephone, but when Jennifer's baby came early it drove all other considerations from my mind. I expect Mr Skinner's been wondering what's going on.'

'What do you want me to do?'

'I'm sure I'll be able to talk your grandfather round, but in the meantime the cottage will need to be seen to.'

'Seen to?' Stella echoed.

'There are one or two things in the loft that may be of interest to you — letters, photos.' Amy looked speculatively at Stella. 'Could you bear to do it?'

'I'm not prepared to commit to anything without Granddad's agreement.'

'I'll work on him. Now what say we refresh ourselves with a quick swim?' Amy nodded to the circular swimming pool. 'Then Jenny wants you to visit.'

★ ★ ★

Jenny was seated in an armchair by the side of the bed.

'What's this about?' Stella asked, intrigued by the summons.

'I was thinking about what you said regarding your relationship to Blanche, and I think I've come up with the answer.'

Stella waited expectantly.

'Would you be her godmother?' she asked in a rush.

'I'd be honoured,' Stella stuttered.

'I wouldn't want her to lose touch with her English roots, and you're the ideal choice.'

'I'd better start learning Spanish,' Stella replied.

328

'I'll make sure she's bilingual,' Jennifer assured her. 'Now let's go and see what sort of night your goddaughter had — and your first lesson in Spanish starts here. The nurse in charge doesn't speak a word of English. So remember: *Buen Dia* and *Cómo estás*.'

'I can manage that,' Stella said, smiling. 'It's the nappy-changing that might be a challenge.'

Laughing together, the two women made their way out of the ward towards the premature baby unit.

32

Doreen bustled through from Pamela's sitting room. 'I hope you've got photos of the new baby to show us. How's the mother?' She delivered a brisk kiss on Stella's cheek. 'And your grandparents?'

'Everyone's well. What's the latest on Pamela?'

Doreen sniffed. 'She's booked herself into a rest home for a few days.'

'Isn't that a good idea?' Stella asked.

The look on Doreen's face suggested to Stella they were not of one mind. 'So in her absence I intend to start on the spring cleaning.' Doreen rattled her bucket in a meaningful manner.

'Then I'll hole up in the studio,' Stella replied.

Dumping her overnight bag on the floor, Stella dialled Mr Skinner's number. 'Sorry I didn't get back to you earlier,' she explained, 'but I've been in Spain with my grandparents.'

'Mrs Price told you she's putting the property on the market?'

'Yes. She's found somewhere she would like to buy in Spain.'

'I can recommend someone to handle the sale.'

'I need to visit first.'

'Let me look at the schedule.' There was the sound of pages being turned. 'We have a potential cancellation. I'll chase it up.'

Finishing her call, Stella checked her emails. There were no new commissions. A newsflash on her home page announced that Mark Dashwood and Kaylee had married in a secret ceremony on a remote Hawaiian island. The picture showed them dancing in the sand with clear blue water lapping their ankles. *We're so happy* was the caption under Kaylee's photograph. 'It was love at first sight,' Mark was quoted as saying.

Rory appeared in the doorway. 'Mind

if I join you? I didn't dare brave the house. There were vigorous cleaning noises emerging from the depths of the glory hole.'

'Doreen's on a roll,' Stella explained.

'Are you free for the rest of the day?'

'It depends what you have in mind.'

'My vintage car needs a run. We could visit my mother. See you outside in ten minutes?'

Swathes of cow parsley swiped the sides of the car as they bowled along. It was difficult to keep up a conversation against the background engine noise and the rushing wind. Stella clung to the door handle with one hand and her scarf with the other. Apart from the odd protest when Rory changed gear, the car didn't let them down and they arrived at the rest home in good time.

'Darlings,' Pamela greeted them. 'Stella, I hear you've been to Spain.'

Rory gestured to his mobile. 'Call coming through. I'll take it outside.'

'I understand Rory blamed you for what happened to me.' Pamela lowered her voice. 'It wasn't your fault.'

'You shouldn't have tried to answer the telephone.'

'I hate being inactive, and things will get a lot busier when June returns.'

'That's what I wanted to talk to you about.' Stella could see Rory's shadow in the corridor as he took his call. 'My grandparents are selling their cottage in Devon and they've asked me to oversee the sale.'

'What are you saying, exactly?'

'After that my plans are fluid.'

'You're leaving us,' Pamela said in a flat voice.

'I think it would be for the best.'

'Have you mentioned anything to Rory?'

'Not yet.'

A nursing assistant opened the door with a tray of tea, and Stella heard Rory finishing off his call.

Rory returned to the room. 'That was June. She and Andrew hope to be back in time for the school presentation.'

'You do still intend taking the photos,

don't you, Stella?' Pamela asked.

Rory cast a questioning look at Stella.

'Of course,' Stella replied firmly.

33

'Good heavens,' Doreen said as she adjusted her bifocals, 'isn't that Henry Lowring again?' She passed the newspaper to Stella.

'Art expert denies fraud,' Stella read the headline.

'Art expert indeed. The only thing he was expert at was charming his way out of trouble.'

'I wonder where he is now,' Stella mused.

'Gone into hiding, most likely.' Doreen raised her teacup. 'May you live in interesting times, Henry.' She took the newspaper back and folded it up. 'Now, on to other things. Pamela and I need some space, so I'm going home to Scotland.' She cast Stella a sideways glance. 'What are your plans?'

'I've been commissioned to take the summer presentation pictures for Mr

Wolff,' Stella began.

'And then what?'

'In the short term I'll be relocating to Devon to sort out the sale of my grandparents' cottage.'

'You must give me the address,' Doreen insisted. 'We mustn't lose touch. Here's the taxi,' she said at the sound of a car arriving in the forecourt. 'Pamela's home.' She began putting on her coat. 'I hope this is only a temporary goodbye.'

It was then Stella noticed the suitcase lodged behind the kitchen door. 'You're leaving now?'

'I thought I made it clear.' Doreen opened the door for Pamela. The two sisters greeted each other briefly before Doreen passed her baggage over to the driver, instructing him to take care not to scuff her suitcase. She offered Stella a brief kiss on the cheek. 'I'd best be going. I don't want to miss my flight.' Before Stella realised what was happening, Doreen was seated in the taxi and it was pulling out of the courtyard.

Pamela sat down at the kitchen table. 'Is there any tea left?' she asked. 'Isn't this nice, just the two of us? It's what I originally intended, but somewhere along the way our plans seem to have gone off track.'

★　★　★

Rory arrived home unexpectedly during the afternoon with Tom and an excited Cheryl in tow.

'We've got a special project to complete,' Tom announced, 'and Mr Wolff said we could have an extended leave for the afternoon to work on it in private.'

'If it's convenient,' Cheryl interceded, an anxious look on her face. She was wearing one of Fenella's treasured butterfly slides in her newly styled hair.

'What a pretty blouse,' Stella said.

Cheryl glowed under Stella's praise. Now she and Tom had joined forces and Fenella was making an effort to be her friend, Cheryl looked much happier.

'Off you go. I'll call you when tea is ready.' Tom and Cheryl disappeared upstairs.

'Have you seen this?' Stella picked up Doreen's newspaper.

'My team and I are now out of the loop.' Rory dropped it onto the coffee table. The cushions moved as he shifted towards Stella on the sofa. 'Stella . . . ' he began in a voice heavy with meaning.

'Rory, don't.'

'You don't know what I was about to say.'

Stella took a deep breath. 'After the school presentation I intend moving out of Minster House.'

A frown creased Rory's forehead. 'Why?'

'It's the only sensible option.'

'Because of June and Andrew?'

'They'll need the room.'

'You may be able to fool yourself, but you can't fool me.'

Stella bit her lip. 'You don't understand.'

'Then enlighten me.'

Rory waited patiently, but Stella had no speech prepared. Whatever her feelings for him, she didn't know how to put them into words. In the past her judgement had been seriously flawed. Mark and Rory moved in the same media world, a world where work schedules meant that commitments were often intense and of a fleeting nature. She didn't think Rory was like Mark, but she wasn't prepared to take the chance.

Tom rushed into the room, closely followed by Cheryl. 'We're waiting for our paint to dry. I've texted Mr Wolff. He says we don't have to be back before lights out, so we can stay over for supper.'

'Don't you think it would have been polite to check first with your grandmother?' Rory snapped.

'She's OK about it.' Tom picked up the remote control. The television screen flickered into life as he changed channels to watch his favourite game show.

Cheryl settled down beside him, and soon they were both laughing at the comedian cracking inane jokes to the sound of canned applause. Still looking annoyed, Rory stood up.

'Shall I do the school run?' Stella offered.

'It's not your problem,' Rory responded briefly. He retrieved his mobile from his pocket as it signalled an incoming call. 'Hello? Doreen. Glad you've arrived safely.' He turned his back on Stella.

'Stella, are you there?' Pamela called downstairs. 'I'm coming down for supper, but I need someone to keep an eye on me.'

'I'll see to my mother.' Rory finished his call. 'And don't worry about supper. I'll make it, then I'll drive Tom and Cheryl back. I'm sure you've got plenty to do.'

Without another glance in her direction, he strode out of the room.

34

After Doreen's departure, Stella and Pamela enjoyed several quiet evenings together in the sitting room. Pamela was eagerly talking about driving again. 'I must thank you for keeping my car on the road,' she said.

'I feel guilty about having used it so much,' Stella replied.

'It's a lot more comfortable than Rory's boneshaker.'

'I shouldn't let him hear you call it that.'

Pamela looked unnaturally serious. 'I worry about him working with live flames.'

Stella remembered how sick she had felt when she found Rory passed out by the side of the car.

'He takes after my late husband,' Pamela continued. 'Billy was forever tinkering around with machinery. After the children came along, I had the perfect excuse not to get involved.'

'Your priorities changed,' Stella said.

'I encouraged my children to be independent. Before she married, June was an air stewardess, and then Rory started work as a roving reporter. I had hoped he would have settled down by now. He's nearly thirty. Don't you think that's a good time to get married?'

Stella fidgeted in her seat. 'I think it's better to be happily single if the right person hasn't come along.'

Pamela sighed and returned her attention to her tapestry. 'I suppose I must learn to be patient and not interfere.'

★　★　★

As the school presentation day grew nearer, Stella began to experience nerves. Mr Wolff had given her a brief tour and explained where the governors and invited guests would be sitting.

'Of course all this will be second

nature to you,' he had said. 'Fenella's been telling us about your awards and how highly your work is regarded. I've told everyone we're very lucky to have such a distinguished photographer in our midst.'

That was when Stella's nerves went into overdrive. Her awards were only minor and not of international standard.

'Is there any special dress code?' she asked Pamela over coffee one evening.

'Some of the older women wear hats. The younger ones try to outdo each other with their designer outfits. I generally opt for a dress and take a jacket in case it turns chilly.'

'Are trousers allowed?'

'I think they are immensely practical. You'll be doing a lot of stretching and bending. What colour is your trouser suit?'

'It's black.'

'I've a lovely silk scarf you can wear to brighten things up. June brought it back from her travels. If you team it up with a white shirt, that should do the trick. Who would have thought Tom and Cheryl would be awarded rosettes for their organic farm project? Such a clever presentation. I understand they're going to get a special mention.' Pamela stuck a needle into her tapestry. 'To think how anxious we were the night Tom disappeared, and how relieved we were when Cheryl's father brought him home and explained where he'd found them.'

'Fenella's been doing well with her horticulture course too,' Stella put in.

'You know, I can't help feeling the children were reluctant to pursue these skills when their mother was around. Something to do with not being cool?' Pamela began rooting around for a new colour of wool. 'June is like Doreen. They're rebels. There are times when the resemblance between them is unmistakeable. I know genetically it's not possible, but that's how I see it.' Pamela's carriage clock chimed the midnight hour. 'Heavens, I had no idea it was so late. Will you take Sparky out, then lock up? We've a big day tomorrow.'

Stella and Pamela intended travelling to the school together the next day.

'I don't know how we're going to get all the children's luggage in the car for the journey home,' Pamela said. 'We may have to leave some behind and collect it later. Such a disappointment June won't be joining us.' She leant on the walking stick she used to steady herself when she was tired. 'See you in the morning.'

Stella stood on the back doorstep, waiting for Sparky to finish prowling around. The inky purple summer night smelt of honeysuckle and Stella inhaled its distinctive sweetness. In the distance she caught the silhouette of an owl as it swooped against the backdrop of a buttermilk moon.

She had again tried broaching the subject of her departure with Pamela, but her response had been to wait until June arrived home. Mr Skinner had assured Stella Fisherman's Cottage would be free over the next four weeks, giving Stella plenty of time to sort things out and to make plans for the future.

'Sparky?' She whistled into the darkness. 'Come on.'

There was the sound of paws tapping on the cobblestones as the dog reappeared from behind a potted plant, growling menacingly.

'What's the matter? You're twitchy tonight.'

A shadow streaked across the courtyard.

'It's only a cat.'

Having seen off the intruder, Sparky trotted obediently into the house and, after one or two more experimental growls, settled in her basket, resting her head on her paws.

'I don't believe we've actually met.'

Stella stumbled against the table as a second shape emerged from the twilight.

'My name is Henry Lowring.'

St Matilda's was a mass of visitors, dignitaries, pupils and parents. With a stomach too unsettled to partake of the buffet lunch, Stella spent the break making sure her equipment was ready. She didn't want anything going wrong at the last minute, and while the auditorium was empty she seized the chance to check the conditions. Natural lighting and humidity could affect her work. She grumbled under her breath about Fenella. If the girl had wanted to look good in front of her classmates she could just as easily have boasted about her own achievements.

Stella was finding it difficult to concentrate as she fumbled with her settings. Her mind was still on last night's encounter with Henry Lowring.

'I'd appreciate it if you didn't scream.' His voice had been silkily polite as he slid into the kitchen. 'And muzzle the dog.'

'How did you get here?' Stella did

her best to quieten Sparky.

'I came over the back way. Knight's Walk used to be part of my old stomping ground. I had hoped Doreen might be here.'

'She's gone back to Scotland.'

'That's a pity.' He slipped his camel-hair coat off his shoulders and draped it over a kitchen chair. 'The thing is,' he began, 'I'm in a spot of difficulty.'

'According to the newspaper you're on the run.'

A look of distaste crossed Henry's face. 'The popular press always blow things out of proportion. I would never do anything as vulgar as going on the run.'

'Then exactly what are you doing?' Stella was determined not to be intimidated.

'Lying low. You have an extremely convenient extension. I'm sure there's space for me there.'

Stella backed away from Henry, hoping Pamela wouldn't hear their voices and come down to investigate. 'You can't stay. Mrs Waugh and her husband are flying home from Dubai and the children break up tomorrow.'

'There's tonight.'

'Rory's using it tonight,' Stella improvised, not sure when Rory was expected back.

'That man is a serious thorn in my flesh. If he hadn't started poking around in things that don't concern him, none of this would have happened.'

'None of this would have happened if you hadn't got involved in the first place.'

'The authorities can't prove anything.'

'There's photographic evidence.'

Henry's complexion bore the evidence of too much good living, and his colour now heightened as a nasty expression crossed his face. 'I was coming to that. Those pictures you took . . . '

'I don't have them.'

Any remaining traces of pleasantness left Henry's face. 'That I find hard to believe.'

'Believe it or not, it's the truth.'

'When I catch someone taking my photograph without my permission, not once but twice, and then I discover that very same person is living with an investigative reporter who is conducting an in-depth inquiry into my activities, I begin to grow a little suspicious.'

'I'm not living with Rory Loates.'

'This is his mother's house.'

'Stella?' Pamela's voice floated down the stairs. 'Who are you talking to?'

'I suggest you leave now.' Stella cast an anxious glance over her shoulder. 'Before I call the police. I can't hold the dog much longer,' she said as Sparky strained against Stella's grip on her collar.

'I want those photos, and nothing's going to stop me getting them,' Henry threatened from the doorway. 'You needn't think you've heard the last of this.'

His buttonhole flower fluttered to the ground as he whipped his coat off the chair. Sparky pounced and mangled the white petals into a soggy mess before spitting them out in disgust.

'That's exactly how I feel.' Stella removed the stalk from Sparky's mouth and threw it in the rubbish bin.

Later, after she had convinced Pamela she had only been talking to Sparky, Stella realised she had been foolish to underestimate Henry. He was in a tight corner, and like all cornered animals he was ready to lash out.

Mr Thomas the art teacher bore down on Stella, snapping her thoughts back to the present. 'There's a search party on the lookout for you. If you're ready, Mr Wolff wants to say a few words of welcome. By the way, this is your lucky day — there's a reporter from the local newspaper here, but his photographer's gone sick so it's your show. You've got free rein to take all the pictures you want. Come on, it's this way.'

Pamela was seated in the front row of the audience and she waved to Stella, who took up her position at the side of the stage. The reporter was scribbling frantically as each name was read out.

Fenella and Tom accepted their

certificates, the former with a newly attained poise, the latter with a cheeky smile at the camera, arm in arm with an equally delighted slimmed-down Cheryl.

'Hope you don't mind my asking,' the local reporter accosted Stella as the proceedings began to wind down, 'but if you could send your best pictures to the newspaper office, we would like to use them. I'll make sure you get the credit and an appropriate fee. I can probably get them syndicated too.'

'I'll need to obtain family permission first,' Stella advised him.

'No problem.' He snapped his note-pad shut. 'Better get back and try to make some sense of my notes. Be seeing you.'

'Yoo hoo, darlings,' a voice called over as everyone spilled out into the grounds.

'Mum.' Fenella was still pink with pleasure as June enveloped her in a hug. 'You made it.'

'Sorry for the late arrival. Got held up by security at the airport. Then we had to scoop up Rory from the station; but we're all here now. Stella, good to see you. Isn't Ma looking brilliant?'

'Did you see us get our awards?' Tom demanded.

'I did indeed. I had no idea I had such talented children.'

Stella drew June to one side as the children ran off in search of their father. 'Can I have a quick word?'

'Goodness, you're looking serious, Stella. Is something wrong? Thanks for all you've done for the children, by the way. I like Tom's new girlfriend. I understand they both want to be vets. Where on earth did that idea come from? And as for Fenella and flowers . . . Sorry,' she apologised, 'I'm talking too much. What was it you wanted to say?'

'Will you be able to get the children's luggage into your car?'

June pulled a face. 'I thought the idea was that you and Ma would help out with the honours. The children have accumulated a lot of stuff during the term and we have to clear everything out to make way for the summer school.'

'If Rory could drive your mother back, I'm sure he would help out. I've got something urgent I need to do.' Now was not the time to explain about Henry Lowring.

'Can't it wait?' June demanded.

'Not really. Besides, you need some family time, and Minster House is going to be rather crowded until things are sorted out.'

'Hmm.' June looked thoughtful. 'You do have a point. But what's the hurry?'

'If I'm quick, I should be able to grab a lift with the local reporter.'

'What are you up to?' June demanded.

'I have to go away.'

'For good?'

'For a while.'

'Is this anything to do with Rory?'

'No,' Stella insisted.

'I suppose you know what you're doing.'

Stella spied the reporter getting into

his car. 'Will you say goodbye to everyone for me?'

'You haven't told me where you're going,' June called out.

'I'll be in touch,' Stella promised and, running after the startled reporter, flagged him down before jumping into his passenger seat.

As they approached the school gates, Stella caught a glimpse of Rory. She ducked her head, but the passenger mirror showed he was standing on the verge staring after them as the car swept past him and out into the road.

35

Stella flung her equipment into the boot of her car then scooted across to the house. Taking the stairs two at a time, she flung open her wardrobe door and threw her clothes into her bags as quickly as she could. Later when the fuss had died down, Stella would contact Pamela personally; but for the moment she couldn't take the risk of Henry Lowring stalking the house in search of his incriminating photos. Now that Andrew was home, and with Rory on the premises, any further unscheduled visits from Henry could be dealt with by the men. But as it was Stella he was after, it was best she made her presence scarce.

She zipped up her bag and hurried onto the landing. A figure emerged from the kitchen.

'What is going on?' Rory demanded.

'I'm leaving.'

'I'd worked that one out for myself.'

'Now June and Andrew are back there isn't space for me here.'

'What about my mother?' Rory demanded in a voice Stella barely recognised. 'Doesn't she deserve better treatment than this?'

'I'll make it up to her, I promise.'

As Stella faced Rory she knew how his victims must feel when they were the targets of his investigations.

'I think it's a good idea you're leaving.'

'You do?' Stella stopped, feeling as though she had been slapped in the face.

'Your timing could have been better, but since you moved in life at Minster House has lurched from one crisis to another.'

'It was my life that went from one crisis to another,' Stella retaliated.

'I don't disagree with you.'

'Then you've no right to accuse me.'

'Of what?'

'Sneaking out.'

'Isn't that exactly what you're doing?' He looked down at the bag Stella had dropped at his feet.

Bandying words with Rory would get Stella nowhere, and if she stayed much longer she feared she might divulge the true reason she was leaving.

'I've made my plans, so if you would please stand aside I'll be on my way.'

'Not before I've had my say.' He took a step towards her. Imprisoned against the stairs, Stella grasped the banister rail to stop herself from toppling backwards. 'I don't know what your motivation is, but I know you're not telling me the complete truth.'

'I haven't time to go into it now.' Stella attempted to move him on, but Rory was as solid as a brick wall.

'I can't flatter myself that I'm the cause of your sudden departure.'

'Please, Rory,' she begged, 'you have to let me go.'

'Not until you tell me exactly what's going on.'

'Nothing's going on,' she insisted, turning her head, unable to meet the inquisition in his eyes.

'Would I be right in suspecting you think my family might be in danger?'

Stella snapped back to face him. 'Whatever gave you that idea?' she gasped.

'Has Henry Lowring been threatening you again?' He put out a hand and clamped it around Stella's arm.

She sagged towards him in defeat. 'He was here last night,' she admitted.

'Why on earth didn't you say something?' Rory demanded.

'There was no one I could tell.'

'What was he doing here?'

'Looking for refuge.'

'He's got a nerve.'

'He started on about the photos. I told him I didn't have them but he didn't believe me.'

'How did you manage to get rid of him?' Rory asked.

A reluctant smile crossed Stella's face. 'I threatened him with you.'

'Good one.' Rory released his hold on her arm. 'So now we have the truth, there's no need for you to leave.'

'Supposing Henry comes back?'

'He won't. He'll suspect you've contacted the authorities and that the premises could now be under surveillance.'

'Is working under cover always like this?' she demanded.

'I've never involved my family. Why on earth did you have to take his wretched photo in the first place?'

Stella began to protest but Rory's mobile signalled an incoming message. He glanced briefly at the screen. 'June can't get the luggage into their people carrier. I'm wanted back at the school.'

'I'd best be going. Thank your mother for everything for me. She's been very kind.'

'I'd rather you told her yourself.' His mobile bleeped again. Stifling a gesture of exasperation, he turned away from her.

At Stella's feet Sparky whined and

put out a paw to detain her. 'I've got to go,' she said gently, her voice catching in her throat. The trusting brown eyes looked up at her and nearly melted her resolve. 'You've got the family to look after now,' she said to the dog. 'Make sure they don't spoil you.' A warm tongue licked her fingers. In the background Stella could hear Rory engaged in animated conversation. She picked up her suitcase and, seizing her chance, walked out of the house before Rory could finish his call.

36

Stella's eyes were gritty with fatigue by the time she reached the golf club car park.

The steward paused by the gates. 'I was about to close up.'

'Am I too late to book in?'

'There's always room for you.'

'I'll settle up in the morning,' she promised. She trundled her luggage down the hill. Mrs Johnson's net curtains twitched as she registered her arrival.

Stella flung open the back windows of the cottage before telephoning Mr Skinner. 'Sorry to disturb you so late,' she said, 'but I've arrived at the cottage. I didn't want you receiving reports of a break-in.'

'I'll call round some time tomorrow,' he promised.

Despite her long journey, Stella was

awake early the next morning and on her second cup of coffee when he arrived.

'I've spoken to my contact and he's happy to handle the sale. He'll send someone along to take photos later.'

'I shall miss the old place,' Stella admitted.

'Actually I have some news of my own,' Mr Skinner said. 'I've decided to retire.'

'Why?'

'The character of the village is changing. That business with the rogue tenants upset my wife, and the job isn't what it used to be.'

Stella had to agree that the status of some of the incomers was causing disquiet among the locals. Wine bars were opening up in place of the craft shops and the mini-market stocked exotic foods, ignoring fresh local produce.

'The gallery that used to showcase local talent has been bought out by an incomer down from London,' Mr Skinner went on. 'I feel it's lost its individualism, but I suppose one must move with the times.'

'I hope Fisherman's Rest won't be priced above the market rate,' Stella said. 'I wouldn't like to think of someone making an easy profit at the expense of the community.'

'I agree.' Mr Skinner finished his coffee. 'I wanted to tell you my plans before you heard the news from another quarter. I'm confident you will have things sorted out by the time I finally sign off, but for the moment it's business as usual.'

After he'd gone Stella decided to tackle the loft. Amy had removed most of the rubbish, but tucked away under a faded bedspread Stella spied a leather suitcase. Inside she found a photograph album and two landscapes. Leaving the suitcase to be disposed of at a later date, Stella clambered back down the loft steps.

The landscapes were heavy and the frames of a surprisingly good quality. One was a seascape showing a fishing boat battling against the elements. The waves were high and angry, and the power of the brush strokes highlighted the emotions of the crew as they fought the forces of nature.

The second painting was a gentler scene, a rural farm with rolling pastures in the background. A horse ploughed a field in straight lines, the farmer guiding the reins and the tiller. A dog bounded along beside them. In the distance a plump woman was carrying a basket of food towards a group of men sharpening scythes. Both artworks reflected men at work, and the vibrancy of colour and attention to detail brought the pictures to life.

It was a shame the gallery had changed hands, she thought. The old proprietor had a vast knowledge of local art and would have been able to advise Stella about them. While she was still debating what to do, there was a knock on the door.

'I'm from the estate agent's,' the man on the doorstep introduced himself.

Stella asked him in and he produced a tape measure from his pocket.

'These bijou properties are very popular,' he enthused as he took measurements. 'I'm getting a lot of interest from clients wanting something substantial but not too big. There's nothing as solid as bricks and mortar, I always say.'

'I wouldn't want the price to be ramped up,' Stella advised him.

'You have no need to worry, Miss Bates. I've already got a young couple in mind. I've been on the lookout for something for them for a while. They're relations of my wife's sister. This cottage would suit them down to the ground.' He gathered up his paperwork. 'With your permission I'll speak to them tonight.'

After he'd gone Stella decided to settle her account with the golf club. Waving to Mrs Johnson, who was sweeping her front step, she hurried up the hill.

'I hear your grandparents are selling

up and that Mr Skinner is retiring,' the secretary said as he issued Stella a parking receipt. 'The character of the village is changing. Suddenly we're fashionable. I suppose it's good for the economy, but I can't help missing the old days.' He smiled at Stella. 'Which makes me sound incredibly ancient.'

'Not at all,' Stella retaliated. 'You're only as old as you feel.'

'How do you feel about lunch? We've fresh trout on the menu.'

'I'm going to have to pass,' she said regretfully. 'Do you know anything about the new gallery owner?' she asked.

'His name is Richard Russell. There's a rumour doing the rounds that he's a failed artist. He's worked wonders with the gallery. It was looking a little tired. Why are you interested in him?'

'I found some paintings in the loft and I'd like to know a little about them.'

The secretary glanced at his watch. 'You should catch him there now. He keeps the shop open at lunchtime. He's diversified into gifts cards and painting materials in an effort to attract the passing trade.'

Stella bundled the paintings into her car and drove to the parking area at the rear of the shop.

'Thought I heard activity,' a man in his thirties greeted her. 'Richard Russell. Are those for me?' He relieved Stella of her load and led the way inside. 'Watch your footing. I save the soft lights and potted plants for front of house.' He placed the paintings on a small table. 'Sorry, I don't know your name.'

'Stella Bates.'

'Pleased to meet you. I'm the new boy in town, but I'm doing my best to fit in. What can I do for you?'

'I found these paintings in the attic of my grandparents' cottage,' she began.

'And you'd like an independent assessment? I can do that for you.' He inspected them with a magnifying glass. 'They're in need of a good clean.'

'Perhaps you could see to that too?'

'My pleasure. And now that the business side of things is over, please take a seat.' He poured out two cups of China tea and nudged a plate of fancy biscuits towards Stella. 'Lunch?' he asked with a friendly smile.

At the front of the shop an assistant was busy assisting two customers with the purchase of some painting materials. The telephone began to ring.

'Why don't you look round?' Richard invited.

Discreet music played in the background, and an elegant water feature created a restful corner for those who wished to take the weight off their feet. A painting was highlighted on an easel in the window. Stella craned her neck to look, then felt as though she had been punched in the stomach.

Richard came up behind her. 'I can't help feeling this lady has quite a past. You can see it in her eyes. I'd date it as mid-nineteenth century French; and I'd say, judging by the delicate detail of the fine lace of her sleeves, that she's of the nobility.'

'Where did you get it?' Stella gasped.

'A customer brought it in.'

'Did he have a white rose in his buttonhole?'

Richard frowned. 'Yes he did. Don't tell me it's a copy.'

37

June answered the telephone. 'Rory's not here. Where are you?'

'Devon,' Stella replied.

'Then you'd best stay there for a while,' June advised. 'You're not very popular here at the moment. What made you run off? You know, I got the blame. Everyone seemed to think I'd upset you. Fenella and Tom didn't speak to me for days. Andrew's gone off looking for work because his job offer fell through, and Ma's shut herself away in her sitting room saying we make too much noise. Some homecoming this has turned out to be. Mr Wolff's been on the telephone as well. He wants you to know your photos are the best he's ever seen, and if you're interested he can put more work your way. Not that you deserve it, deserting us without a word.'

'June,' Stella cut her short, 'I need to contact Rory.'

'He's been like a bear with a sore head ever since you left. He's done nothing but work on that wretched car of his. Every night he's out there banging away, then testing the engine at all hours. It's driving us mad. When I complained he snapped my head off. I wasn't having any of that, and before I knew it we were at it hammer and tongs.'

'June,' Stella raised her voice above hers, 'do you have the number of Rory's flat?'

'I do.'

'Can I have it please?' Stella asked through clenched teeth.

'He's not there.'

'Where is he?'

'Not sure. We had another row after his exhaust blew up, and he stormed off. We're not on speaking terms at the moment. Hang on. I think I did hear him mention something about America. Have you tried his mobile number?'

'It's switched off.'

'It sounds like he's out of the country then, doesn't it? Want me to pass on a message when he gets back?' Now she'd had her say, June sounded in a more reasonable frame of mind.

'If it's not too much trouble,' Stella replied.

'As usual someone's made off with the telephone pad. Hold on.' She was back after a brief pause. 'I've borrowed a pencil off Tom. He sends his love and says he hates you. Right, now what do you want to say to my brother that's so urgent?'

Stella took a deep breath. With her butterfly attention to detail, June would not have been her first choice for communication; nevertheless, she dictated the message. 'You will make sure to pass it on, won't you?'

'I'll do my best,' June replied with an edge to her voice. 'I can't say fairer than that, can I?'

'Tell him . . . ' Stella paused. 'I've seen a painting in a local gallery.'

'Is that it?'

'Yes.'

'Why all the fuss?'

'I wasn't sure when I first saw it.'

'That it was a painting?'

'It's too complicated to explain over the telephone.'

'You can say that again.'

'Just tell Rory that our suspicions about Charles were correct.'

'Just a minute.' Stella clenched her fists as June bellowed at her son, 'Have you got another pencil, Tom? This one's broken. Right, where were we? Art gallery, suspicions were correct. Go on.'

'There was a painting on an easel, and I'm sure we saw the original in Charles's château in France. It's Marie.'

'And that's all?' June sounded perplexed.

'The gallery owner identified Henry Lowring from his buttonhole.'

'Wasn't he one of Doreen's old flames?'

'Yes.'

'Might have known she'd be at the bottom of it somewhere.'

'Can you make sure Rory gets the message?' Stella pleaded.

'I'll do my best,' June trilled. There was a loud burst of music in the background. 'I've got to zap that noise. Ma's trying to sleep. Bye.'

★ ★ ★

Over the next week there was no further contact from Richard Russell or Rory, and Stella was forced to come to the conclusion that Rory was no longer interested in art fraud — or her.

She began scanning advertisements for positions offering accommodation with light household duties. Closing down her laptop, she glanced out of the window. The rain had cleared and she needed a breath of fresh air. She decided to walk up to the gallery to see what progress Richard had made with her paintings.

Marie's picture was no longer on its stand. Richard had looked confused when Stella shrugged off her suspicions

375

with a light laugh.

'I've probably seen a photo of this painting somewhere,' she bluffed.

'And the man with the rose in his buttonhole?' Richard frowned.

'Again, I think I'm getting confused. You'll let me know about my grandmother's paintings?'

She left Richard staring after her with a puzzled frown.

Today a man she didn't recognise emerged from the back room. 'I'm only standing in for the day. I'll ask Richard to contact you when he gets back,' he promised.

At a loose end, Stella crossed the road into the bakery. Inside it was warm and steamy.

'Be with you in a moment,' Sid called over. 'Got to get a batch of buns out of the oven.'

'I'm in no hurry.' Stella rubbed steam off the window to see what was going on outside. A sharp shower had sent shoppers scurrying for cover. Rain bounced off the pavement and formed oily puddles in the road. A bright beam of sunlight broke through the clouds, temporarily blinding Stella. As she blinked the black spots from her eyes there was a loud screech of brakes, followed by raised voices.

'Sorry,' a pedestrian apologised, 'the sunlight dazzled me.'

The pedestrian adjusted his coat over his shoulders and attempted to cross the road for a second time. A flower fluttered to the ground. It was a crushed white rose.

'Now then, Stella.' Sid emerged from the back of the shop. 'Can I interest you in the last of our crab sandwiches, or is it something sweet you're after?' He slipped her an extra cream bun. 'Don't tell Doris,' he said with a wink.

Stella raised the collar of her jacket to hide her face as she emerged from the bakery. She didn't dare glance across to the gallery. The rain had eased off, but there was no sign of Henry or his wretched camel-hair coat. She had to get away before he spotted her.

A shadow touched her shoulder as she approached the cottage. She screamed and whirled round.

'Sorry, didn't mean to startle you.'

'Doreen?' Stella felt faint with relief as the older woman hugged her.

'You did say I could visit any time I liked. So here I am.' She let Stella go and grabbed her paper bag. 'What's in here? More crab sandwiches? What are we doing standing around in the wet? Get the kettle on.'

38

'You didn't rely on June to pass on your message, did you?' Doreen didn't wait for a reply. 'Still, we don't need Rory. We can manage on our own. Now what was all that about Henry Lowring running around in a thunderstorm shedding petals left, right and centre?'

'I'm not sure it was him now.' Stella hesitated. 'The bakery windows were fogged up.'

'Your eyesight's perfect. It was Henry, all right.' Doreen gave a positive nod of her head.

'It seems too much of a coincidence that I should be down here at the same time a copy of Charles's painting of Marie is being displayed in the local gallery, and then Henry should appear.'

'It makes perfect sense. Things were too hot for Henry in his usual haunts. He had to go somewhere.'

'Why here?'

'I don't want to scare you, Stella, but he's got you in his sights. He was down here once before, and that's probably when he discovered your local gallery could be a good outlet for his fakes.'

'It was Mrs Johnson who saw him last time.'

'That woman has eyes that would shame a laser beam,' Doreen said. 'She accosted me, wanting to know what I was up to. Actually, her cup of tea was very welcome.' Doreen paused. 'Where were we?' she asked.

'Discussing Henry's motivation.'

'Right. Well that's my take on it. What do you suggest we do?'

'Nothing,' Stella responded in alarm, registering the light of battle in Doreen's eyes. 'I don't want you taking unnecessary risks.'

Doreen surprised Stella by meekly agreeing with her. 'Perhaps you're right. Henry will want to lie low if the police are after him. Is this art fraud business the only reason you wanted to contact Rory?'

'Yes.'

'No other reason?' Doreen fixed her with a penetrating stare. 'I may be getting on, but I haven't totally lost the plot. He's in love with you.'

'It doesn't mean that I'm in love with him.'

Again, much to Stella's surprise, Doreen gave in. 'Have it your own way. What are we going to do if we're not going to go after Henry?'

'I'm down here to sell my grand-parents' cottage,' Stella said.

'Would you like me to help?'

'I need help getting a suitcase down from the loft.'

'Then I'm your girl, and I'll do any shopping you need too. Just give me a list.'

The next morning, glad to have the chance to be on her own, Stella started to organise her portfolio; something she liked to do every so often. Engrossed in her work, she jumped when Doreen banged on the window. 'The key is dangling on some string through the letter box,' she called out. 'Let yourself in.' She heard the door opening and footsteps in the hall.

'I know you've got those photos, and I want them *now*.' Henry Lowring's voice froze Stella to her chair.

'I told you I haven't got them.'

'And *I* told *you* I don't believe you. In here, are they?' He snatched up her laptop and ducked away from Stella. 'This is heading for the dustbin.'

Suddenly, Henry widened his eyes in pain. He stumbled towards Stella with his arms outstretched, dropped the laptop, and sank to his knees.

'Stay where you are, rat-face. Clobbering you is something I've longed to do for years,' a voice snarled.

'You interfering — ' Henry began.

'I said stay where you are.' Doreen imprisoned his ankle with her foot. 'Vera Johnson's called the police,' she informed Stella.

Stella looked down to Henry, who

was floundering around like an angry fish, then back to a triumphant Doreen.

Taking advantage of Doreen's lapsed attention, Henry rolled onto his knees and caught Doreen off balance. There was a loud crack as her knee came into contact with the wall.

'Stop him!' Stella shrieked at Vera Johnson, who was standing in the doorway.

Henry pushed her to one side and charged out into the street — to the sound of blaring sirens. Police cars raced down the hill, blue lights flashing, and screeched to a halt in front of the cottage.

An excited Vera peered through the net curtains. 'Someone's rugby-tackled that dreadful man. I'm going outside to get a better view. He won't get away.'

'He'd better not. I've a score to settle with him,' Doreen ground out through gritted teeth. She winced as the other woman cannoned into her. 'Watch it, Vera.'

'Has anyone called for an ambulance?'

Stella shouted down the corridor. 'We have an injured lady in here.'

'I don't need an ambulance.' Doreen's robust objection was marred by another grimace of pain. 'Wretched knee. Why did it choose today of all days to play up?'

'Sit down,' Stella told her, dragging a chair across the room.

'What, and miss all the fun?'

'Do as you're told,' Stella ordered.

'Only if you promise to tell me everything later.' Doreen sank gratefully into the high-backed chair.

'Need any help?' A female police officer poked her head through the door.

'My friend's injured her knee.'

'Have you apprehended Mr Lowring?' Doreen demanded as the officer spoke into her two-way radio.

'We have, and it's thanks to you.'

'That's a result, isn't it?' Doreen asked.

'Indeed it is. Sit there until the ambulance arrives. We've had enough heroics for one day.'

Doreen turned to Stella. 'She's bossy,

isn't she? Do you think I should have words with her senior officer?'

'I *am* the senior officer present,' the policewoman retaliated from the hall.

'Think you've met your match,' Stella laughed.

'That's the trouble with females today,' Doreen muttered. 'They don't know their place.'

'I'd say we know it very well, and you're only jealous because it wasn't like that in your day.' Stella retrieved her laptop off the floor.

'Didn't do any damage, did he?' Doreen asked.

'I don't think so.'

Doreen smiled through her pain. 'Vera came up trumps. What's she doing now?'

Stella glanced through the net curtain. 'Having a lovely time being interviewed.'

Doreen groaned.

Stella knelt down in concern. 'Does the swelling hurt?'

'Henry did give it a bash,' Doreen admitted.

'You're going to have one monster

bruise in the morning.'

'If I ever come across him again, he'll have one to match mine.'

Footsteps strode down the hall.

'Rory.' Doreen beamed at her nephew.

Ignoring his aunt, Rory dragged Stella to her feet and crushed her body to his. 'I thought you'd been injured.' He buried his face in her hair.

'She hasn't.' Doreen raised her voice. 'But *I* have.'

Stella wriggled free from Rory's embrace. 'It's her knee. Look, it's swelling up.'

Rory turned on his aunt. 'You probably asked for it.'

'Not long on sympathy, are you?' she retaliated. 'And what took you so long? I telephoned yesterday.'

'I would have been here earlier if I'd known where you'd gone.' He glared at Stella, who glared at Doreen.

'You telephoned Rory?' Stella echoed.

'Somebody had to get the pair of you together,' Doreen said, jutting out her jaw.

A loud cough interrupted them.

'Who exactly is the injured party here?' a paramedic asked as he tramped into the room.

'My aunt,' Rory replied, then drew Stella to one side. 'I told you not to get involved,' he hissed.

'You didn't do any such thing. Besides, you can't tell me what to do.'

'No,' Rory was forced to agree, 'I can't, can I?'

Another flush of colour flooded Stella's face. She didn't think it was possible to turn any redder. 'June told me you were in America.'

'There are times when I could strangle my sister. I was actually in Wales.'

'Don't take it out on June.'

'Only twice in my life have I had to cancel an important interview, and both times it was your fault.'

Another loud cough interrupted them. 'I'm going to have to take Mrs Soames to the hospital,' the paramedic announced.

'It's Miss, young man,' Doreen

interrupted him. 'I have never married, but even if I had I would have retained my maiden name, and I do not want to go to hospital.'

'Your knee needs dressing,' he insisted.

'And my aunt will do as she's told,' Rory insisted. 'If she doesn't, I'm sending her back to Scotland.'

Doreen opened her mouth to protest, then thought better of it.

'Come along, *Miss* Soames.' Then he added in a softer voice, 'We'll soon have you striding around again telling everyone what to do.'

Rory placed an arm around Stella's shoulders. 'Do you think the golf club will be able to put me up for the night?' he asked. 'You and I have unfinished business.'

39

Later that evening Stella walked up the hill to the golf club. Rory was waiting for her in the lounge.

'I've booked a table for eight o'clock,' he explained.

Stella accepted a glass of wine from the steward before they sat down in a secluded corner. For a few moments neither of them spoke.

It was Rory who first broke the silence. 'It's been a hectic day.'

'You should have seen Henry's face when Doreen came at him from behind. I wish I'd had my camera.'

'I expect Henry will sing like a canary. He's the sort of person who'll take everyone down with him.'

'What do we do now?' Stella asked, wondering why she was feeling so flat.

The dress code for the main restaurant in the golf club was smart casual and Rory was wearing tailored trousers, his outdoor tan emphasised by a crisp white open-necked shirt.

'I propose we forget about family, art forgers and photographs, and talk about us,' he said.

'Haven't we said it all?' Stella's heart trebled its beat.

'I know we've been through everything several times, but these last few days have been hell — and I'm not talking paintings.'

The expression in Rory's brown eyes was making Stella feel uncomfortably warm.

He looked at Stella's empty glass. 'Would you like another?'

'Could you make it an orange juice? I need to keep a clear head if I'm going to understand what's going on.'

'I had no idea what was going on between us, and to make matters worse I was stuck in Wales.'

'Rory — ' Stella got no further.

'The thing is,' Rory carried on as if she hadn't tried to interrupt, 'my work involves mixing with the grittier side of life — you see what I'm trying to say?'

'I have no idea,' Stella admitted.

'I'm always standing around in boiling hot or freezing cold places wondering why I didn't choose to work in a comfortable office and push paper around a desk.'

Stella relished the tart taste of her ice-cold orange juice on her tongue.

'You know Charles is married, don't you?' Rory said.

'You've already told me that,' Stella replied, 'and I took it on board the first time.'

'He's in serious trouble, if you were entertaining any hopes in that direction.' He snatched up his tankard of beer. 'Mark's married too.'

'That's not news to me either.'

'And as for that Frenchman who was old enough to be your father — Montmartre?' Rory jogged Stella's memory.

'Pierre?' Stella stifled a laugh. 'I thought he was charming, didn't you?'

'He's another one with a string of

female friends.' He signalled for a second drink, and like Stella he made it an orange juice. 'June's husband has found a new job,' he told her.

Stella decided to give up following the thread of Rory's conversation. The best course of action, she decided, was to agree with everything he said until something eventually made sense. 'I hope you're not going to suggest I'm involved with Andrew too.'

'What I'm telling you is they'll be moving out of Minster House next month.'

'And you want me to move back in as Pamela's companion?'

'No.'

Stella hadn't been looking forward to finding somewhere new to live, and for a very short moment she had hoped it wouldn't be necessary.

'Is she still annoyed with me for leaving so suddenly?' Stella asked, awash with guilt.

'The whole family is furious with you. June got it in the neck from Fenella and Tom because they thought she'd upset you. When Doreen found out what you'd done she accused me of behaving badly. And my mother did something I've never known her do before.'

'What?' Stella asked with a frisson of alarm.

'She sulked. She wouldn't speak to anyone for days.'

'I only did what I did because I thought Henry would come looking for me and I didn't want to endanger your family.'

'You didn't think to ask us first?'

'I took the coward's way out,' Stella admitted.

Rory's voice softened. 'You're not a coward. I don't think I've ever met anyone as brave as you.'

'You said I was foolhardy.'

'I said a lot of things.'

Rory caressed Stella's hand. His touch made Stella's fingers tingle.

'Talking of Andrew, he was another one who got roped into the drama. He hadn't a clue what was going on. At one point he threatened to return to Dubai unless the family calmed down.'

'Well, it's all sorted now.' Stella smiled brightly, changing the subject. 'Shall we order? I'm starving.'

'You're going to have to curb your appetite,' was Rory's brisk reply. He waved away a hovering waiter. 'I haven't finished all I want to say.'

'In that case, could I have some nibbles?'

With an impatient gesture at the waiter, Rory ordered a bowl of nuts and some crisps. When they arrived, Rory cupped half the contents of the bowl of crisps in his hand and munched steadily before brushing salt off his trousers. His seemed reluctant to look Stella in the eye.

'Rory?' Stella prompted, putting a hand on his thigh. 'Is something wrong?'

'How do you fancy living at Minster House?'

'You just said you didn't want me there.'

'No I didn't.'

Stella closed her eyes. She was

beginning to get a headache.

'My mother can't live in the house on her own.'

'But you don't want me there as her companion.'

'I want you living there as my wife.'

Stella's peanuts bounced all over the table and onto the carpet. The waiter leapt forward. Rory moved the bowl of crisps out of Stella's reach.

'You are now supposed to look starry-eyed and flutter your eyelashes at me. Peanuts don't normally figure in the scene.'

'In your dreams,' Stella retaliated. 'And give me those crisps. They're mine.'

The waiter reappeared with another dish of peanuts. A bubble of laughter rose in Stella's chest. She delved into her bag for a tissue and blinked away tears of laughter.

'Was that why you were warning me off Charles and Pierre and Mark?'

Rory eyed up the crisps as if he wished they could come up with an explanation.

Stella decided to put him out of his misery. 'Look . . . Do you promise not to interfere in my professional life?'

'No.'

'Right, well I promise not to always be around to cook supper.'

'I don't suggest we engage Doreen as housekeeper.'

'Not a good idea,' Stella agreed solemnly.

'Can I take all this as a yes?' Rory asked deftly, moving the second bowl of crisps away from Stella's outstretched hand.

'One more thing,' she stipulated.

'Yes?'

'Can we go to Paris for our honey-moon?'

We do hope that you have enjoyed reading this large print book.

Did you know that all of our titles are available for purchase?

We publish a wide range of high quality large print books including:
Romances, Mysteries, Classics
General Fiction
Non Fiction and Westerns

Special interest titles available in large print are:
The Little Oxford Dictionary
Music Book, Song Book
Hymn Book, Service Book

Also available from us courtesy of Oxford University Press:
Young Readers' Dictionary
(large print edition)
Young Readers' Thesaurus
(large print edition)

For further information or a free brochure, please contact us at:
Ulverscroft Large Print Books Ltd.,
The Green, Bradgate Road, Anstey,
Leicester, LE7 7FU, England.
Tel: (00 44) 0116 236 4325
Fax: (00 44) 0116 234 0205

Other titles in the
Linford Romance Library:

A LITTLE LOVING

Gael Morrison

Jenny Holden fell in love with Matt Chambers, the local high school football star. When she fell pregnant, he didn't believe the baby was his. Now a pro player, he is back in town to attend the wedding of his best friend, who is also Jenny's boss. And when he sees Jenny's son Sam, the boy's parentage is unquestionable. Jenny, now a widow, knows all Sam wants is a father — his real father. But can she trust the man who once turned his back on them?

MISTS OF DARKNESS

Rebecca Bennett

Who tried to kill TV producer Zannah Edgecumbe by pushing her over a cliff? The answer is hidden somewhere in her slowly returning memory. Is it cameraman Jonathan Tyler, her aggressive and passionate fiancé, or is it Matthew Tregenna, the handsome but remote doctor treating her — the man with whom she is falling in love? She remembers Hugh, the boy she adored as a child — but where is he now? Lost in an abyss of blurred and broken memories, Zannah must return to the cliff-top to discover the horrifying truth.

A QUESTION OF LOVE

Gwen Kirkwood

As a partner in Kershaw & Co., Roseanne has very clear plans for her career and her life. She is fiercely independent, and has no time for anything outside of work — until she meets Euan Kennedy, the nephew of her business partner, Mr Kershaw. Euan is funny, warm, charming — and drop-dead gorgeous. But when Euan doubts Roseanne's integrity, the feelings that have started to grow between them are dashed. How can she ever love a man who thinks so little of her?

A HERO'S WELCOME

Jasmina Svenne

Wounded during the American War of Independence, all Robert Lester wants is to return home to Nottinghamshire. But when he arrives, feverish and drenched by a storm, he finds his mother and sister missing and an attractive stranger living in their cottage. Ellen Fairfax, a young widow with a small son, offers him shelter for the night. But Ellen is hiding from her past, and her act of kindness puts all that is most precious to her in jeopardy . . .

SAFE HARBOUR

Natalie Kleinman

Working as a hostess on a cruise ship, Beth Walker meets Ryan Donovan, and is drawn to his soft Irish lilt and mischievous eyes. It's love at first sight, each swept away by the other like the waves on the sea. But when Beth learns of a dark secret Ryan's been harbouring, she feels her only choice is to break it off and never see him again. Despite the misery it causes them, it looks like her plan will work — until she discovers she is carrying Ryan's child . . .